The farther north Jacklyn drove, the more restless Dillon became.

He'd hoped the years had changed him, had at least taught him something about himself. But this place brought it all back. The betrayal. The anger. The aching need for vengeance.

"I'm sorry, where did you say we were going?" he asked. Jack, of course, hadn't said.

"Your old stompin' grounds," she said.

That's what he was afraid of. They'd gone from the motel to pick up a horse trailer, horses and tack. He couldn't wait to get back in the saddle. He was just worried where that horse was going to take him. Maybe more to the point, what he would do once he and Jack were deep in this isolated country, just the two of them.

B.J. DANIELS

BIG SKY STANDOFF

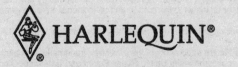

HARLEQUIN®

TORONTO • NEW YORK • LONDON
AMSTERDAM • PARIS • SYDNEY • HAMBURG
STOCKHOLM • ATHENS • TOKYO • MILAN • MADRID
PRAGUE • WARSAW • BUDAPEST • AUCKLAND

This one is for Harry Burton Johnson Jr. Who knows
how different our lives would have been had you lived.

ISBN-13: 978-0-373-88743-9
ISBN-10:   0-373-88743-4

BIG SKY STANDOFF

ABOUT THE AUTHOR

B.J. Daniels's life dream was to write books. After a career as an award-winning newspaper journalist, she sold thirty-seven short stories before she finally wrote her first book. That book, *Odd Man Out*, received a 4½-star review from *Romantic Times BOOKreviews* and went on to be nominated for Best Harlequin Intrigue of 1995. Since then she has won numerous awards, including a career achievement award for romantic suspense.

B.J. lives in Montana with her husband, Parker, two springer spaniels, Spot and Jem, and an aging, temperamental tomcat named Jeff. When she isn't writing, she snowboards, camps, boats and plays tennis.

To contact B.J., write to her at P.O. Box 1173, Malta, MT 59538, e-mail her at bjdanielsmystery@hotmail.com or check out her Web site at www.bjdaniels.com.

Books by B.J. Daniels

CAST OF CHARACTERS

Dillon Savage—The rustler had a few plans of his own when the woman who'd put him in prison broke him out for a special assignment.

Jacklyn Wilde—She was gambling her career—and her life—by teaming up with the charming cattle rustler.

Shade Waters—The elderly rancher was about to do something that he knew could get him killed.

Nate Waters—The son of the richest rancher in central Montana, he wanted the one thing he couldn't seem to get—his father's respect.

Sheriff Claude McCray—He had his reasons for wanting to see Dillon Savage back in prison, and one of them was a woman.

Tom Robinson—The rancher was hanging on by a thread. If he lost any more cattle he would go under.

Buford Cole—The ranch hand had been as close to Dillon Savage as anyone.

Halsey Waters—His death had left a hole in a lot of people's lives.

Arlen Dubois—He had a habit of talking too much. But then again, no one listened, so what did it hurt?

Pete Barclay—The cowboy was a lousy liar. But was that all?

Chapter One

Dillon Savage shoved back his black Stetson and looked up at all that blue sky as he breathed in the morning. Behind him the razor wire of the prison gleamed in the blinding sunlight.

He didn't look back as he started up the dirt road. It felt damn good to be out. Like most ex-cons, he told himself he was never going back.

He had put the past behind him. No more axes to grind. No debts to settle. He felt only a glimmer of that old gnawing ache for vengeance that had eaten away at him for years. An ache that told him he could never forget the past.

From down the road past the guardhouse, he saw the green Montana state pickup kicking up dust as it hightailed toward him.

He shoved away any concerns and grinned

to himself. He'd been anticipating this for weeks and still couldn't believe he'd gotten an early release. He watched the pickup slow so the driver could talk to the guard.

Wouldn't be long now. He turned his face up to the sun, soaking in its warmth as he enjoyed his first few minutes of freedom in years. Freedom. Damn, but he'd missed it.

It was all he could do not to drop to his knees and kiss the ground. But the last thing he wanted was to have anyone know how hard it had been doing his time. Or just how grateful he was to be out.

The pickup engine revved. Dillon leaned back, watching the truck rumble down the road and come to a stop just feet from him. The sun glinted off the windshield in a blinding array of fractured light, making it impossible to see the driver, but he could feel the calculating, cold gaze on him.

He waited, not wanting to appear overly anxious. Not wanting to get out of the sun just yet. Or to let go of his last few seconds of being alone and free.

The driver's side door of the pickup swung open. Dillon glanced at the ground next to the truck, staring at the sturdy boots that stepped

out, and working his way up the long legs
wrapped in denim, to the firearm strapped at
the hip, the belt cinched around the slim waist.
Then, slowing his eyes, he took in the tucked-
in tan shirt and full rounded breasts bowing
the fabric, before eyeing the pale throat. Her
long dark hair was pulled into a braid. Finally
he looked into that way-too-familiar face
under the straw hat—a face he'd dreamed
about for four long years.

Damn, this woman seemed to only get
sexier. But it was her eyes that held his attention, just as they had years before. Shimmer-
ing gray pools that reminded him of a high
mountain lake early in the year, the surface
frosted over with ice. Deeper, the water was
colder than a scorned woman's heart.

Yep, one glance from those eyes could
freeze a man in his tracks. Kind of like the
look she was giving him right now.

"Hi, Jack," he said with a grin as he tipped
his battered black Stetson to her. "Nice of
you to pick me up."

STOCK DETECTIVE Jacklyn Wilde knew the
minute she saw him waiting for her beside
the road that this had been a mistake.

Clearly, he'd charmed the guards into letting him out so he could walk up the road to meet her, rather than wait for her to pick him up at the release office. He was already showing her that he wasn't going to let her call the shots.

She shook her head. She'd known getting him out was a gamble. She'd foolishly convinced herself that she could handle him.

How could she have forgotten how dangerous Dillon Savage really was? Hadn't her superiors tried to warn her? She reminded herself that this wasn't just a career breaker for her. This could get her killed.

"Get in, Mr. Savage."

He grinned. Prison clearly hadn't made him any less cocky. If she didn't know better, she'd think this had been his idea instead of hers. She felt that fissure of worry work its way under her skin, and was unable to shake the feeling that Dillon Savage had her right where he wanted her.

More than any other woman he'd crossed paths with, she knew what the man was capable of. His charm was deadly and he used it to his advantage at every opportunity. But knowing it was one thing. Keeping Dillon

Savage from beguiling her into believing he wasn't dangerous was another.

The thought did little to relieve her worry.

As she slid behind the wheel, he sauntered around to the passenger side, opened the door and tossed his duffel bag behind the seat.

"Is that all your belongings?" she asked.

"I prefer to travel light." He slid his long, lanky frame into the cab, slammed the door and stretched out, practically purring as he made himself comfortable.

She was aware of how he seemed to fill the entire cab of the truck, taking all the oxygen, pervading the space with his male scent.

As she started the truck, she saw him glance out the windshield as if taking one last look. The prison was small by most standards—a few large, plain buildings with snow-capped mountains behind them. Wouldn't even have looked like a prison if it wasn't for the guard towers and razor-wire fences.

"Going to miss it?" she asked sarcastically as she turned the truck around and headed back toward the gate.

"Prison?" He sounded amused.

"I would imagine you made some good friends there." She doubted prison had taught him anything but more ways to break the law. As if he needed that.

He chuckled. "I make good friends wherever I go. It's my good-natured personality." He reached back to rub his neck.

"Was it painful having the monitoring device implanted?" A part of her hoped it had given him as much pain as he'd caused her.

He shook his head and ran his finger along the tiny white scar behind his left ear. "Better anyday than an ankle bracelet. Anyway, you wanted me to be able to ride a horse. Can't wear a boot with one of those damn ankle monitors. Can't ride where we're going in tennis shoes."

She was willing to bet Dillon Savage could ride bare-ass naked.

His words registered slowly, and she gave a start. *"Where we're going?"* she asked, repeating his words and trying to keep her voice even.

He grinned. "We're chasing cattle rustlers, right? Not the kind who drive up with semi-trucks and load in a couple hundred head."

"How do you know *that?*"

He cocked his head at her, amusement in his deep blue eyes. "Because you would have caught them by now if that was the case. No, I'd wager these rustlers are too smart for that. That means they're stealing the cattle that are the least accessible, the farthest from the ranch house."

"It sounds as if you know these guys," she commented as the guard waved them past the gate.

Dillon was looking toward the mountains. He chuckled softly. "I'm familiar with the type."

As she drove down the hill to the town of Deer Lodge, Montana, she had the bad feeling that her boss had been right.

"What makes you think a man like Dillon Savage is going to help you?" Chief Brand Inspector Allan Stratton had demanded when she told him her idea. "He's a *criminal*."

"He's been in prison for four years. A man like him, locked up..." She'd looked away. Prison would be hell for a man like him. Dillon was like a wild horse. He needed to run free. If she understood anything about him, it was that.

"He's dangerous," Stratton had said. "I shouldn't have to tell you that. And if you really believe that he's been masterminding this band of rustlers from his prison cell...

Then getting him out would accomplish what, exactly?"

"He'll slip up. He'll have to help me catch them or he goes back to prison." She was counting on this taste of freedom working in her favor.

"You really think he'll give up his own men?" Stratton scoffed.

"I think the rustling ring has double-crossed him." It was just a feeling she had, and she could also be dead wrong. But she didn't tell her boss that.

"Wouldn't he be afraid of them implicating him?"

"Who would believe them? After all, Dillon Savage has been behind bars for the past four years. How could he mastermind a rustling ring from Montana State Prison? Certainly he would be too smart to let any evidence of such a crime exist."

"I hope you know what you're doing," Stratton said. "For the record, I'm against it." No big surprise there. He wasn't going down if this was the mistake he thought it was. "And the ranchers sure as hell aren't going to like it. You have no idea what you're getting yourself into."

Stratton had been wrong about that, she

thought, as she glanced at Dillon Savage. She'd made a deal with the devil and now he was sitting next to her, looking as if he already had her soul locked up.

She watched him rub the tiny scar behind his left ear again. It still surprised her that he'd agreed to the implanted monitoring device. Via satellite, she would know where he was at any second of the day. That alone would go against the grain of a man like Dillon Savage. Maybe she was right about how badly he'd wanted out of prison.

But then again, she knew he could very well have a more personal motive for going along with the deal.

"So the device isn't giving you any discomfort?" she asked.

He grinned. "For a man who can't remember the last time he was in a vehicle without shackles, it's all good."

As she drove through the small prison town of Deer Lodge, past the original jail, which was now an old west museum, she wondered what his life had been like behind bars.

Dillon Savage had spent his early life on his family's cattle ranch, leaving to attend university out East. Later, when his father sold the ranch, Dillon had returned, only to start stealing other people's cattle. Living in the wilds, with no home, no roots, he'd kept on the move, always one step ahead of her. Being locked up really must have been his own private hell.

Unless he had something to occupy his mind. Like rustling cattle vicariously from his prison cell.

"I'm surprised you didn't work the prison ranch," she said as she drove onto Interstate 90 and headed east.

"They worried that their cattle would start disappearing."

She smiled not only at his attempt at humor, but also at the truth of the matter. It had taken her over two years to catch Dillon Savage. And even now she wasn't sure how that had happened. The one thing she could be certain of was that catching him had little to do with her—and a whole lot to do with Dillon. He'd messed up and it had gotten him sent to prison. She'd just given him a ride.

REDA HARPER STOOD at the window of her ranch house, tapping the toe of her boot impatiently as she cursed the mailman. She was a tall, wiry woman with short-cropped gray hair and what some called an unpleasant disposition.

The truth? Reda Harper was a bitch, and not only did she take pride in it, she also felt justified.

She shoved aside the curtain, squinting against the glare to study her mailbox up on the county road. The red flag was still up. The mailman hadn't come yet. In fact, Gus was late. As usual. And she knew why.

Angeline Franklin.

The last few weeks Angeline had been going up the road to meet mailman Gus Turner, presumably to get her mail. By the time Angeline and Gus got through gabbin' and flirtin' with each other, Reda Harper's mail was late, and she was getting damn tired of it.

She had a notion to send Angeline one of her letters. The thought buoyed her spirits. It was disgraceful the way Angeline hung on that mailbox, looking all doe-eyed, while Gus stuttered and stammered and didn't have the sense to just drive off.

The phone rang, making Reda jump. With a curse, she stepped away from the window to answer it.

"Listen, you old hateful crone. If you don't stop—"

She slammed down the receiver as hard as she could, her thin lips turning up in a whisper of a smile as she went back to the window.

The red flag was down on her mailbox, the dust on the road settling around the fence posts.

Reda took a deep breath. Her letters were on their way. She smiled, finally free to get to work.

Taking her shotgun down from the rack by the door, she reached into the drawer and shook out a half-dozen shells, stuffing them into her jacket pocket as she headed to the barn to saddle her horse.

A woman rancher living alone had to take care of herself. Reda Harper had had sixty-one years of practice.

"I WANT TO MAKE SURE we understand each other," Jacklyn Wilde said, concentrating on her driving as an eighteen-wheeler blew past.

"Oh, I think we understand each other perfectly," Dillon commented. He was looking out at the landscape as if he couldn't get enough of it.

A late storm had lightly dusted the tops of

the Boulder Mountains along the Continental Divide to the east. Running across the valley, as far as the eye could see, spring grasses, brilliantly green, rippled in the breeze, broken only by an occasional creek of crystal clear water.

"I got you an early release contingent on your help. Any misstep on your part and you go back immediately, your stay extended." When he said nothing she looked over at him.

He grinned again, turning those blue eyes on her. "We went over this when you came to the prison the first time. I got it. But like I told you then, I have no idea who these rustlers are. How could I, given that I've been locked up for four years? But as promised, I'll teach you everything I know about rustling."

Which they both knew was no small thing. Jacklyn returned her gaze to her driving, hating how smug and self-satisfied he looked slouched in her pickup seat. "If at any time I suspect that you're deterring my investigation—"

"It's back to the slammer," he said. "See, we understand each other perfectly." He tipped his Stetson down, his head cradled by the seat, and closed his eyes. A few moments later he appeared to be sound asleep.

She swore softly. While she hadn't created the monster, she'd definitely let him out of his cage.

DILLON WOKE WITH A START, bolting upright, confused for an instant as to where he was.

Jacklyn Wilde had stopped the truck in a lot next to a café. As she cut the engine, her gaze was almost pitying.

"Prison makes you a light sleeper." He shrugged, damn sorry she'd seen that moment of panic. Prison had definitely changed his sleep patterns. Changed a lot of things, he thought. He knew the only way he could keep from going back to jail was to keep the upper hand with Ms. Wilde. And that was going to be a full-time job as it was, without her seeing any weakness in him.

"Hungry?" she asked.

He glanced toward the café. "Always." It felt strange opening the pickup door, climbing out sans shackles and walking across the open parking lot without a guard or two at his side. Strange how odd freedom felt. Even freedom with strings attached.

He quickened his step so he could open the restaurant door for her.

Jacklyn shot him a look that said it wasn't

going to be *that* kind of relationship. He knew she wanted him to see her as anything but a woman. Good luck with that.

He grinned as she graciously entered, and he followed her to a booth by the window as he tried to remember the last meal he'd had on the outside. Antelope steak over a campfire deep in the mountains, and a can of cold beans. He closed his eyes for a moment and could almost smell the aroma rising from the flames.

"Coffee?"

He opened his eyes to find a young, cute waitress standing next to their table. She'd put down menus and two glasses of water. He nodded to the coffee and made a point of not letting Jacklyn see him noticing how tight the waitress's uniform skirt was as he took a long drink of his water and opened his menu.

"I'll have the chef salad," Jacklyn said when the waitress returned with their coffees.

Dillon was still looking at his menu. It had been four years on the inside. Four years with no options. And now he felt overwhelmed by all the items listed.

"Sir?"

He looked up at the waitress and said the first thing that came to mind. "I'll have a burger. A cheeseburger with bacon."

"Fries?"

"Sure." It had been even longer since he'd sat in a booth across from a woman. He watched Jack take off her hat and put it on the seat next to her. Her hair was just as she'd worn it when she was chasing him years ago—a single, coal-black braid that fell most of the way down her slim back.

He smiled, feeling as if he needed to pinch himself. Never in his wildest dreams did he ever think he'd be having lunch with Jacklyn Wilde in Butte, Montana. It felt surreal. Just like it felt being out of prison.

"Something amusing?" she asked.

"Just thinking about what the guys back at the prison would say if they could see me now, having lunch with Jack Wilde. Hell, you're infamous back there."

She narrowed her gaze at him, her eyes like slits of ice beneath the dark lashes.

"Seriously," he said. "Mention the name Jacklyn Wilde and you can set off a whole cell block. It's said that you always get your man, just like the Mounties. Hell, you got me." He'd always wondered how she'd managed it. "How exactly *did* you do that?"

He instantly regretted asking, knowing it was better if he never found out, because he'd had four long years to think about it. And he knew in his heart that someone had set him up. He just didn't know who.

"I'll never forget that day, the first time I came face-to-face with you," he said, smiling to hide his true feelings. "One look into those gray eyes of yours and I knew I was a goner. You do have incredible eyes."

"One more rule, Mr. Savage. You and I will be working together, so save your charm for a woman who might appreciate it. If there is such a woman."

He laughed. "That's cold, Jack, but like I said, I understand our relationship perfectly. You have nothing to worry about when it comes to me." He winked at her.

Jack's look practically gave him frostbite.

Fortunately, the waitress brought their lunches just then, and the burger and fries warmed him up, filling his belly, settling him down a little. He liked listening to the normal sounds of the café, watching people come and go. It had been so long. He also liked watching Jacklyn Wilde.

She ate with the same efficiency with which she drove and did her job. No wasted energy. A single-minded focus. He hadn't entirely been kidding about her being a legend in the prison. It was one reason Dillon was so damn glad to be sitting across the table from her.

He'd been amazed when she'd come to him with her proposition. She'd get him out of prison, but for his part, he had to teach her the tricks of his trade so she could catch a band of rustlers who'd been making some pretty big scores across Montana. At least that was her story.

He'd seen in the papers that the cattlemen's association was up in arms, demanding something be done. It had been all the talk in the prison, the rustlers becoming heroes among the cellies.

What got to him was that Jack had no idea what she was offering him. He hadn't agreed at first, because he hadn't wanted to seem too eager. And didn't want to make her suspicious.

But what prisoner wouldn't jump at the chance to get out and spend time in the most isolated parts of Montana with the woman who'd put him behind bars?

"Where, exactly, are we headed?" he asked after he'd finished his burger. He dragged his last fry through a lake of ketchup, his gaze on her. It still felt so weird being out, eating like a normal person in a restaurant, sitting here with a woman he'd thought about every day for four years.

Her gray eyes bored into him. "I'd prefer not to discuss business in a public place."

He smiled. "Well, maybe there's something else you'd like to discuss."

"Other than business, you and I have nothing to say to each other," she said, her tone as steely as her spine.

"All right, Jack. I just thought we could get to know each other a little better, since we're going to be working together."

"I know you well enough, thank you."

He chuckled and leaned back in the booth, making himself comfortable as he watched her finish her salad. He could tell she hated having his gaze on her. It made her uneasy, but she did a damn good job of pretending it didn't.

He'd let her talk him into the prerelease deal, amused by how badly she'd wanted him out of prison. She needed to stop the rustlers, to calm the cattlemen, to prove she could do her job in a macho man's West.

Did she suspect Dillon's motives for going along with the deal? He could only speculate on what went through that mind of hers.

She looked up from her plate, those gray

eyes cold and calculating. As he met her gaze, he realized that if she could read his mind, it would be a short ride back to prison.

She said nothing, just resumed eating. She was wary, though. But then, she had every reason to be mistrustful of him, didn't she.

Chapter Two

Rancher Shade Waters looked across the table at his son, his temper ready to boil over—lunch guest or not.

In fact, he suspected Nate had invited her thinking it would keep Shade from saying anything. He hadn't seen his son in several days, and then Nate had shown up with this *woman*.

"I suppose you heard," Shade said, unable to sit here holding his tongue any longer. "Another ranch was hit last night by that band of rustlers. If they don't catch those sons of—"

"Do we always have to talk ranch business at meals?" Nate snapped. "You're ruining everyone's appetite."

Nate's appetite seemed to be fine, and Shade couldn't have cared less about Morgan Landers's. From what he could tell, she ate like a bird. Their guest was like most of the women his son dated: skinny, snobby and greedy. He'd seen the way she'd looked around the ranch house. As if taking inventory of the antiques, estimating their worth at an auction.

Shade had no doubt what Morgan Landers would do with the ranch and the house if she got the chance.

But then, he wasn't about to let her get her hands on either one.

"Please don't mind me," Morgan said. "This rustling thing is definitely upsetting."

"No one can stop them. They've fooled everyone and proved they're smarter than the ranchers and especially that hotshot stock inspector, Wilde," Nate said, clearly amused by all of it.

"I beg your pardon?" Shade snapped, no longer even trying to keep his temper under control. How could his son be so stupid? "You sound like you admire these thieves."

"Well, they haven't hit our ranch, so what do you care?"

Shade was speechless. He'd never understood his son, but it had never crossed his mind that Nate was just plain stupid.

He heard his voice rising as he said, "As

long as those men are out there stealing cattle, this ranch is at risk. I won't rest until they are all behind bars. And as for the man who's leading this ring, I'd like to see him hanged from that big tree down by the creek, like he would have been if your grandfather was still alive."

Nate chuckled and looked at Morgan, the two sharing a private joke. "As if he can be caught."

"Do you know something I don't?" the rancher asked between gritted teeth.

"The leader of the rustlers is already behind bars," Morgan said. "Everyone knows it's Dillon Savage. Who else could it be?"

"Really?" Shade looked at his son.

"Who else *could* it be?" Nate said. He had the irritating habit of parroting everything Morgan said.

"Well, for your edification, Dillon Savage is not behind bars anymore. Jacklyn Wilde got him out of prison."

Nate had the sense to look surprised—and worried. "Why would she do that?"

"Supposedly to help her catch the rustlers. Isn't that rich?" Waters said, and swore under his breath.

Nate looked upset, but Shade doubted his

concern was for their cattle. No, he thought, looking over at the woman beside his son, Nate had other worries when it came to Dillon Savage.

"The whole damn thing was kept quiet," Shade said, fighting his anger. "For obvious reasons." He would have fought it tooth and nail had he known.

"Like I said, do we have to talk about this now?" Nate asked pointedly.

"Your *guest* might have more of an interest in the topic than you think," he replied. "After all, she was Dillon Savage's..." he looked at Morgan as if he wasn't sure what to call their relationship "...girlfriend."

Nate shot him a warning look as the cook came in with another basket of warm rolls. Morgan was picking at her salad. It galled Waters that while he and Nate were having beefsteaks, Morgan had opted for rabbit food. The woman was dating a cattle rancher, for hell's sake.

The rancher cursed under his breath, angry at his son on so many levels he didn't even know where to begin. Nate not only looked like his mother—blond with hazel eyes, and an aristocratic air about him—he'd also gotten her softness, something Shade had tried to "cowboy" out of him, although, regretfully, he hadn't succeeded.

He wished he hadn't let Nate's mother spoil the boy so. Now in his early thirties, Nate stood to inherit everything Shade had spent his life building. Nate had no idea the sacrifices his father had made, the obstacles he'd had to overcome, the things he'd had to do. Still had to do. Nate, like his mother, would have been shocked and repulsed if he'd known.

Fortunately, Elizabeth had always turned a blind eye to anything her husband did, although Shade wondered if it wasn't what had put her in an early grave. That and the loss of her firstborn son, Halsey.

While Halsey had loved everything about ranching, Nate never took to it. And just the thought of ever turning the W Bar over to him was killing Shade.

Nate leaned toward Morgan now, whispering something in her ear that made her chuckle coyly—and turned Shade's stomach.

"I'm sorry, Morgan, is talk of Dillon Savage making you uncomfortable?" he asked innocently.

Nate shot him a warning look.

"It's all right, Nate," she said, smiling at the older Waters. "Yes, I knew Dillon…well."

Her smile broadened. "Do I care that he's out of prison? Not in the least. Dillon and I were over a long time ago."

Shade looked at his son to see if he believed any of that bull. Nate had never had any sense when it came to women. Apparently, he was buying everything Morgan told him, probably because he had a good view of the woman's breasts in that low-cut top.

"Then you didn't write him while he was in prison or go see him?" Shade asked, ignoring the look his son gave him.

"No," Morgan said, her smile slipping a little. "We'd gone our separate ways long before Dillon went to prison."

She was lying through her teeth. He suspected that she'd been keeping Dillon up on everything going on in the county, especially at the W Bar.

"Well," Shade said, with exaggerated relief, "I guess the only thing Nate and I have to worry about with Savage out is losing our cattle." He dug into his steak as he noted with some satisfaction that his son had lost *his* appetite.

AS JACKLYN WILDE DROVE east past one small Montana town after another, Dillon realized he didn't have any idea where they were headed or what she had planned for him.

But that was the idea, wasn't it? She wanted to keep him off balance. She didn't want him to know too much—that had been clear from that first day she'd come to see him in prison.

He glanced over at her now. Back when she'd been trying to catch him rustling, he'd known only what he'd heard about her. It wasn't until he'd come face-to-face with her and the gun she had leveled at him that he'd looked into her steel-gray eyes and realized everything he'd heard about her just might be true.

She was relentless, clever and cunning, cold and calculating. Ice water ran through her veins. In prison, anyone who'd crossed her path swore she was tougher than any man, but with a woman's sense of justice, and therefore more dangerous.

He couldn't argue the point, given that she was the one who'd put him behind bars.

"So when are you going to tell me the real reason you got me out?" he asked now.

Outside the pickup, the landscape had changed from mountains and towering, dark green pines to rolling hills studded with sagebrush. Tall golden grasses undulated like waves in the breeze and the sky opened up, wide and blue from horizon to horizon. It truly was Big Sky Country.

"I thought I made myself clear on that point," she said, keeping her eyes on the road. "You're going to help me catch rustlers."

He chuckled and she finally looked over at him. "Something funny about that?"

"You didn't get me out of prison to catch rustlers. You are perfectly capable of catching any rustler out there and we both know it." He met her gray eyes. In this light, they were a light silver, and fathomless. The kind of eyes that you could get lost in. But then the light changed. Her gaze was again just a sheet of ice, flat and freezing.

"I need your expertise," she said simply.

Right. "Well, I'll be of little help to you if you keep me in the dark," he said, smiling wryly as he changed tactics. "Unless you have something besides rustling on your mind. I mean, after what happened the first time we met…"

Her eyes narrowed in warning. "The only reason you aren't still behind bars is because you were good at rustling. That's the only talent of yours I'm interested in."

He lifted a brow, still smiling. "That's too bad. Some of my other talents are even more impressive. Like my dancing," he added quickly. He could see she hadn't expected that was where he was headed.

"I'm surprised you had the time, given how busy you were stealing other people's cattle."

He shrugged. "All work and no play… What about you, Jack? What do you do for fun?"

"Mr. Savage, I told you, our discussions will be restricted to business only."

"If that makes you more comfortable… How about you tell me where we're headed then, Jack."

"You'll be updated on a need to know basis, Mr. Savage, and at this point, the only thing you need to know is that I'm Investigator Wilde or Ms. Wilde. Not Jack."

"Still Ms., huh? I guess it's hard to find a cowboy who's man enough to handle a woman like you."

Her jaw tightened, but she didn't take the bait.

He gazed out the windshield, enjoying himself. There were all kinds of ways to get even, he realized. Some of them wouldn't even get him sent back to prison.

Too bad he'd so often in the past four years revisited the day she'd caught him. It was like worrying a sore tooth with his tongue. He'd lost more than his freedom that day.

There'd been only one bright spot in his capture. After she'd cuffed him, he'd stumbled forward to steal one last thing: a kiss.

He'd taken her by surprise, just as she had him with the capture. He'd thought about that kiss a lot over the years. Now, as he glanced over at her, he wondered if he'd be disappointed if he kissed her again. *When* he kissed her again, he thought with a grin. And he *would* kiss her again. If only goodbye.

"Is there a problem, Mr. Savage?" she asked.

"Naw, just remembering the day you caught me," he said, and chuckled.

"Lewistown," she said irritably, making him laugh. "We're headed for Lewistown."

"Now that wasn't so hard, was it?" The center of the state. A hub of cattle ranches. How appropriate, given that rustlers had run rampant there back in the 1800s. It had gotten so bad that some ranchers took matters into their own hands. On July 4, 1884, a couple of suspected rustling ringleaders, "Longhair" Owen and "Rattlesnake Jake" Fallon, were busy shooting up the town when a band of vigilantes gunned them down in the street. Longhair Owen took nine bullets and Rattle-snake Jake eleven.

Dillon wondered how long it would be before a band of vigilantes started shooting first and asking questions later, given how upset the ranchers were now over this latest ring of rustlers. Was that why Jack had gotten him out? Was she hoping some ranchers would string him up?

Staring out at the landscape, he knew that the only reason she'd told him where they were headed was because he wouldn't be getting an opportunity between here and there to call anyone and reveal their destination.

"Your lack of trust cuts me to the core," he said as he ran his finger along the tiny scar behind his left ear, where the chip was embedded under his skin.

Much like Jacklyn Wilde had gotten under his skin and been grating on him ever since. He told himself he'd be free of both before long. In the meantime, he tried not to think about the fact that Jack as well as her superiors would know where he was at any given moment.

"You sure that monitoring chip isn't bothering you?" she asked, frowning at him.

He hadn't realized she'd been watching him. Apparently she planned to keep a close eye on him—as well as monitor his every move.

"Naw," he said, running his finger over the scar. "I'm good."

Her look said he was anything but, and they both knew it.

SHADE WATERS always made a point of walking up the road to the mailbox after lunch, even in the dead of winter.

While it was a good half mile to the county road and he liked the exercise, his real motive was to get to the mail before anyone else did.

The letters had been coming for years now. He just never knew which day of the week, so he always felt a little sick as he made the hike up the road.

Even after all this time, his fingers shook a little as he pulled down the lid and peered inside. The envelope and single sheet of stationery within were always a paler lavender, as if the paper kept fading with the years.

Today he was halfway up the ranch lane when he saw Gus come flying down the county road, skidding to a stop and almost taking out the mailbox.

"What the hell?" Waters said under his breath as he watched the carrier hurriedly sort through the mail, open the box and stuff it inside. He had been running later and later recently.

Gus saw him, gave a quick wave and sped off almost guiltily.

Waters shook his head, already irritated knowing that his son and Morgan Landers were back at the house together. He had to put an end to that little romance. Maybe Dillon Savage being out of prison would do the trick.

At least something good would come of Savage being on the loose again.

When Shade finally reached the mailbox, he stopped to catch his breath, half dreading what he might find inside. Fingers trembling, he pulled down the lid, his gaze searching for the pale lavender envelope as he reached for the mail.

Even before he'd gone through the stack, he knew the letter hadn't come. A mixture of disappointment and worry washed over him as he slammed the box shut. He hadn't realized how much he anticipated the letters. What if they stopped coming?

He shook his head at his own foolishness,

wondering if he wasn't losing his mind. What
man looked forward to a blackmail letter? he
asked himself as he tucked the post under his
arm and headed back up the lane.

JACKLYN HAD JUST LEFT the town of Judith
Gap when her cell phone rang and she saw
with annoyance that it was her boss. She
glanced over at Dillon, wishing she didn't
have to take the call in front of him, because
more than likely it would be bad news.

"Wilde."

"So how did it go?" Stratton asked, an edge
to his voice. He was just waiting for things
to go badly so he could say I told you so.

"Fine," she said, and glanced again at Dillon.
He was chewing on a toothpick, stretched out
in the seat as if he was ready for another nap.

"I hope you aren't making the biggest
mistake of your career. Not to mention your
life," Stratton said.

So did Jacklyn. But they'd been over this
already. She waited, fearing he was calling to
tell her the rustlers had hit again. She knew
he hadn't phoned just to see how she was
doing. Stratton, too, had a receiver terminal
that told him exactly where Dillon Savage

was at all times. Which in turn would tell her boss exactly where she was, as well.

"Shade Waters wants to see you," Stratton said finally.

She should have known. Waters owned the W Bar, the largest ranch in the area, and had a habit of throwing his weight around. "I've already told him I'm doing everything possible to—"

"He's starting what he calls a neighborhood watch group to catch the rustlers," Stratton said.

"Vigilante group, you mean." She swore under her breath and felt Dillon Savage's gaze on her.

"Waters has all the ranchers fired up about Savage being released. He's got Sheriff McCray heading up a meeting tomorrow night at the community center. I want you there. You need to put a lid on this pronto. We can't have those ranchers taking things into their own hands. Hell, they'll end up shooting each other."

She groaned inwardly. There would be no stopping Waters. She'd already had several run-ins with him, and now that he knew about her getting Dillon Savage out of prison, he would be out for blood. Hers.

"I'll do what I can at the meeting." What choice did she have? "Will you be there as well?"

"I'm not sure I can make it." The chicken. "You do realize by now that you've opened up a hornets' nest with this Savage thing, don't you?" He hung up, but not before she'd heard the self-satisfied "I told you so" in his voice.

DILLON WATCHED JACK from under the brim of his Stetson, curious as to what was going on. Unless he missed his guess, she was getting her butt chewed by one of her bosses. He could just imagine the bureaucratic bull she had to put up with from men who sat in their cozy offices while she was out risking her life to protect a bunch of cows.

And from the sounds of it, the ranchers were doing exactly what he'd expected they would—forming a vigilante group and taking the law into their own hands. This situation was a geyser ready to go off. And Dillon had put himself right in the middle of it.

He watched her snap shut the phone. She squared her shoulders, took a deep breath and stared straight ahead, hands gripping the wheel as she drove. He knew she was desperate. Hell, she wouldn't have gotten him out of prison if she hadn't been. She'd stuck her neck out and she would have to be a fool not to realize she was going to get it chopped off.

For a split second, he felt sorry for her. Then he reminded himself that Jacklyn Wilde was the enemy. And no matter how intriguing he found her, he would do well to remember that.

"Everything all right?" he asked innocently.

She shot him a look that said if he wanted to keep his head he wouldn't get smart with her right now.

Unfortunately, he'd never done the smart thing. "Why do you do it?"

"What?" she snapped.

"This job."

She seemed surprised by the question. "I *like* my job."

He scoffed at that. "Putting up with rich ranchers, not to mention your arrogant bosses and all that bureaucrat crap?"

"I'm good at what I do," she said defensively.

"You'd be good at anything you set your mind to," he said, meaning it. She was smart, savvy, dedicated. Plus her looks wouldn't hurt. "You could have any job you wanted."

"I like putting felons behind bars."

"You put *cattle rustlers* behind bars," he corrected. "Come on, Jack, most people see rustling as an Old West institution, not a felony. Hell, it was how a lot of ranchers in the old days built their huge spreads, with a running branding iron, and a little larceny in their blood. Rustling wasn't even a crime until those same ranchers started losing cattle themselves."

"Apparently that's an attitude that hasn't changed for two hundred years," she snapped. "Rustling, with all its legends and lore." She shook her head angrily, her face flushed. "It's why rustlers are seldom treated as seriously as burglars or car thieves."

He shrugged. "It comes down to simple math. If you can make ten grand in a matter of minutes easier and with less risk and more reward than holding up a convenience store, you're gonna do it." He could see that he had her dander up, and he smiled to himself, egging her on. "I see it as a form of living off the land."

"It's a *crime*."

He laughed. "Come on, everyone steals."

"They most certainly do not." Her hands gripped the wheel tightly, and she pressed her foot on the gas pedal as her irritation rose. He saw that she was going over the speed limit, and grinned to himself.

"So you're telling me that you've never listened to bootleg music?" he asked. "Tried a grape at the supermarket before buying the bunch? Taken a marginal deduction on your taxes?"

"No," she said emphatically.

"You're *that* squeaky clean?" He shook his head, studying her. "So you've never done *anything* wrong? Nothing you've regretted? Nothing you're ashamed of?" He saw the flicker in her expression. Her eyes darted away as heat rose up the soft flesh of her throat.

He'd hit a nerve. Jack had something to hide. Dillon itched to know what. What in her past had her racing down the highway, way over the speed limit?

"You might want to slow down," he said quietly. "I'd hate to see you get a ticket for breaking the law."

Her gaze flew to the speedometer. A curse escaped her lips as she instantly let up on the gas and glared at him. "You did that on purpose."

He grinned to himself yet again as he

leaned back in the seat and watched her from under the brim of his hat, speculating on what secret she might be hiding. Had to have something to do with a man, he thought. Didn't it always?

Everyone at prison swore she was an ice princess, cold-blooded as a snake. A woman above reproach. But what if under that rigid, authoritarian-cop persona was a hot-blooded, passionate woman who was fallible like the rest of them?

That might explain why she was so driven. Maybe, like him, she was running from something. Just the thought hooked him. Because before he and Jacklyn Wilde parted ways, he was determined to find her weakness.

And use it to his advantage.

RANCHER TOM ROBINSON had been riding his fence line, the sun low and hot on the horizon, when he saw the cut barbed wire and the fresh horse tracks in the dirt.

Tom was in his fifties, tall, slim and weathered. He'd taken over the ranch from his father, who'd worked it with *his* father.

A confirmed bachelor not so much by choice as circumstances, Tom liked being alone with his thoughts, liked being able to hear the crickets chirping in the sagebrush, the meadowlarks singing as he passed.

Not that he hadn't dated some in his younger days. He liked woman well enough. But he'd quickly found he didn't like the sound of a woman's voice, especially when it required him to answer with more than one word.

He'd been riding since early morning and had seen no sign of trouble. He knew he'd been pushing his luck, since he hadn't yet lost any stock. A lot of ranchers in this county and the next had already been hit by the band of rustlers. Some of the ranchers, the smaller ones, had been forced to sell out.

Shade Waters had been buying up ranch land for years now and had the biggest spread in two counties. He had tried to buy Robinson's ranch, but Tom had held pat. He planned to die on this ranch, even if it meant dying destitute. He was down to one full-time hired man and some seasonal, which meant the place was getting run-down. Too much work. Not enough time.

On top of that, now he had rustlers to worry about. And as he rode the miles of his fence, through prairie and badlands, he couldn't shake the feeling that his luck was about to run out. This latest gang of rustlers were a brazen bunch. Why, just last month two cowboys had driven up to the Crowley Ranch to the north and loaded up forty head in broad daylight.

Margaret Crowley had been in the house cooking lunch at the time. She'd looked out, seen the truck and had just assumed her husband had hired someone to move some cattle for him.

She hadn't gotten a good look at the men or the truck. But then, most cowboys looked alike, as did muddy stock trucks.

Tom could imagine what old man Crowley had said when he found out his wife had just let the rustlers steal their cattle.

Tom was shaking his head in amusement when he spotted the cut barbed wire. Seeing the set of horseshoe prints in the dirt, he brought his horse up short. He was thinking of the tracks when he heard the whinny of a horse and looked up in time to see a horse and rider disappear into a stand of pines a couple hundred yards to the east.

Tom was pretty sure the rider had seen him and had headed for the trees just past the creek. From the creek bottom, the land rose abruptly in rocky outcroppings and thick stands of Ponderosa pines, providing cover.

"What the hell?" Tom said to himself. He looked around for other riders, but saw only the one set of tracks in the soft earth. He felt his pulse begin to pound as he stared at his cut barbed wire fence lying on the ground at his horse's feet.

Tom swore, something he seldom did. He squinted toward the spot where he'd last seen the rider. This part of his ranch was the most isolated—and rugged. It bordered the Bureau of Land Management on one corner and Shade Waters's land on the other.

The man had to be one of the rustlers. Who else would cut the fence and take to the trees when seen?

Still keeping an eye on the spot where the horse and rider had disappeared, Tom urged his mount forward, riding slowly, his hand on the butt of his sidearm.

Chapter Three

Jacklyn silently cursed Dillon Savage as she drove, glad she hadn't gotten a speeding ticket. Wouldn't he have loved that? It was bad enough she'd proved his point that everyone broke the law.

She couldn't believe she'd let him get to her. Like right now. She knew damned well he wasn't really sleeping. She'd bet every penny she had in the bank that he was over there smugly grinning to himself, pleased that he'd stirred her up. The man was impossible.

She tried to relax, but she couldn't have been more tense if she'd had a convicted murderer sitting next to her instead of a cattle rustler. But then, she'd always figured Dillon Savage was only a trigger pull away from being a killer, anyway.

She could hear him breathing softly, and every once in a while caught a whiff of his all-male scent. With his eyes closed, she could almost convince herself this had been a good idea.

Desperate times required desperate measures. She had her bosses and a whole lot of angry cattlemen demanding that the rustlers be stopped. Because of her high success rate in the past—and the fact that she'd brought in the now legendary Dillon Savage—everyone expected her to catch this latest rustling ring.

She'd done everything she could think to do, from encouraging local law enforcement to check anyone moving herds late at night, to having workers at feedlots and sale barns watch for anyone suspicious selling cattle.

Not surprisingly, she'd met resistance when she'd tried to get the ranchers themselves to take measures to ward off the rustlers, such as locking gates, checking the backgrounds of seasonal employees and keeping a better eye on their stock.

But many of the ranches were huge, the cattle miles from the house. A lot of ranches were now run by absentee owners. Animals often weren't checked for weeks, even months on end. By the time a rancher realized some of his herd was missing, the rustlers were long gone.

Everyone was angry and demanding something be done. But at this point, she wasn't sure anyone could stop this band of rustlers. These guys were too good. Almost as good as Dillon Savage had been in his heyday.

And that was why she'd gotten him out of prison, she reminded herself as she turned on the radio, keeping the volume down just in case he really was sleeping. She liked him better asleep.

Lost in her own private thoughts, she drove toward Lewistown, Montana, to the sounds of country music on the radio and the hum of tires on the pavement. Ahead was nothing but trouble.

But the real trouble, she knew, was sitting right beside her.

DILLON STIRRED as she pulled up in front of the Yogo Inn in downtown Lewistown and parked the pickup.

He blinked at the motel sign, forgetting for

a moment where he was. His body ached from the hours in the pickup, but he'd never felt better in his life.

Opening his door, he breathed in the evening air. A slight breeze rustled the leaves on the trees nearby. He stretched, watching Jack as she reached behind the seat for her small suitcase.

"I can get that," he said.

"Just take care of your own," she replied, without looking at him.

Inside the motel, Dillon felt like a kept man. He stood back as Jack registered and paid for their two adjoining reserved rooms, then asked about places in town that delivered food.

"What sounds good to you?" she asked him after she'd been given the keys, both of which she kept, and was rolling her small suitcase down the hallway.

She traveled light, too, it appeared. But then, he expected nothing less than efficiency from Jack.

"What sounds good to me?" He cocked a brow at her, thinking how long it had been.

"For *dinner*," she snapped.

"Chinese."

She seemed surprised. "I thought you'd want steak."

"We had steak in prison. What we didn't have was Chinese food. Unless you'd prefer something else."

"No, Chinese will be fine," she said as she opened the door to his room.

He looked in and couldn't help but feel a small thrill. It had been years since he'd slept in a real bed. Past it, the bathroom door was open and he could see a bathtub. Amazing how he used to take something like a bathtub for granted.

"Is everything all right?" Jack asked.

He nodded, smiling. "Everything's great." He took a deep breath, surprised how little it took to make him feel overjoyed. "Would you mind if I have a bath before dinner? In fact, just order for me. Anything spicy."

Her look said she should have known he'd want something spicy. "I'll be right next door," she said, as if she had to warn him.

The last thing on his mind was taking off. All he could think about was that bathtub—and the queen-size bed. Well, almost. He looked at Jack. Past her, down the hall, he spotted a vending machine.

"Is there something else?" she asked.

He grinned. "Do you have some change? I'd really like to get something out of the vending machine."

She glanced behind her, then reached into her shoulder bag and handed him a couple of dollars.

"Thanks." He looked down at the money in his hand. He hadn't seen money for a while, either. He tossed his duffel bag into the room and strode down the hallway, knowing she was watching him. From the machine, he bought a soda and, just for the hell of it, a container of sea scent bubble bath.

She was still standing in the hallway, not even pretending she wasn't keeping an eye on him.

"You'll ruin my reputation if you tell anyone about this," he said, only half joking as he lifted the package of bubble bath. "But when I saw that bathtub... We only had showers in prison," he added when he saw her confusion.

"I hadn't realized..."

"It's scary enough in the showers," he said with a shake of his head. "Can't imagine being caught in a bathtub there."

She ducked her head and put her key into

the lock on her room door, as if not wanting to think about what went on in prison. "I'll let you know when our dinner arrives." She opened her door, but didn't look at him. "Enjoy your bath."

He chuckled. "Oh, I intend to."

JACKLYN SWORE as she closed her room door. The last thing she wanted to do was imagine Dillon Savage lounging in a tubful of bubbles.

Bubble bath? Clearly, he didn't worry about his masculinity. Not when he had it in spades. But she knew that hadn't been his reason for buying the bubble bath. He'd wanted her imagining him in that tub.

She opened her suitcase and took out the small receiver terminal with the built-in global positioning system, turning it on just in case the bath had been a ruse. The steady beep confirmed that he was just next door. In fact, she could hear the water running on the other side of the adjoining door.

In the desk drawer, she found a menu for the local Chinese restaurant, and ordered a variety of items to be delivered, all but one spicy. It seemed easier than going out, since after they ate, she wanted to get right down to business.

With luck, she'd be ready when the rustlers struck again.

Her cell phone rang. She checked the number, not surprised that it was her boss again. "Wilde."

"Is he there?"

"No. He's in the adjoining room."

"He's probably using the motel room phone to call his friends and let them know where he is and what your plans are," Stratton said, sounding irritated.

"The phone in his room is tapped," she said. "If he makes a call, he'll be back in prison tomorrow. But he isn't going to call anyone and warn them. I haven't told him anything."

"Good. I didn't want him to hear this," Stratton said. "The rustlers hit another ranch. Bud Drummond's."

The Drummond ranch was to the north, almost to the Missouri River. Jacklyn swore under her breath. "When?"

"He's not sure. He'd been out of town for a few days. When he got back, he rode fence and found where the rustlers had cut the barbed wire and gotten what he estimates was about twenty head."

Less than usual. "Why didn't they get more? Is it possible someone saw them?"

"Doubtful. It's at the north end of his ranch, a stretch along the river," Stratton said. "I told him you were going to be up that way tomorrow, anyway, so you'd stop by."

It had rained the day before. Any tracks would be gone. She doubted there would be anything to find—just like usual.

"Savage giving you any trouble?" Stratton asked.

"No." No trouble, unless you counted the psychological games he played. She had a mental flash of him in the tub, sea scent bubbles up to his neck. Exactly the image she knew Dillon had hoped she'd have when he'd bought the bubble bath.

"I shouldn't have to remind you how clever he is or how long it took you to catch him the last time. Don't underestimate him."

She heard the water finally shut off next door. She checked the monitor. Dillon was exactly where he'd said he would be.

"Trust me," she said, "I know only too well what Dillon Savage is capable of."

TOM ROBINSON DISMOUNTED in the dry creek bottom and pulled out his handgun. He hadn't realized how late it was. He was losing light. A horse whinnied somewhere above him on the hillside. He moved behind one of the large pines and listened, trying to determine if the horseback rider was moving.

He knew the man was still up there. This was the only cover for miles. At the very least he was trespassing. But Tom knew that, more than likely, the rider was one of the rustlers. Since the man was alone, maybe he was just checking out the ranch layout, finding the best access to the cattle in this section of pasture.

Tom had gotten only a glimpse of him, but that glimpse was more than anyone else had gotten of the rustlers. His heart began to pound at the thought of catching the man, being the one who brought down the rustling gang.

He had two options. He could wait for the intruder to break cover and try to make a run for it.

Or he could flush him out.

Leaving his horse, Tom worked his way up the steep incline, taking a more direct route on foot than the horseback rider had. Pebble-size stones rolled under his boots and cascaded down with every step he took.

Halfway up, he stopped, leaning against one of the large rocks to thumb off the safety on his weapon. His hands were shaking. It had crossed his mind belatedly that there might be more than one rider now on his spread. Maybe they'd planned to meet here in the trees. There could be others waiting in ambush at the top of the hill.

He considered turning back, but this was his land and he was determined to defend it and his livestock. He knew he had at least one man cornered. Once he broke from the shelter of trees, Tom would see him. With luck, he would be able to get off a shot. Unless the intruder was waiting for the cover of darkness.

This, Tom knew, was the point where the cops on television called for backup. But even if he'd had a cell phone, he wouldn't have been able to get service out here. Nor could he wait for someone to arrive and help him even if he could call for assistance.

No, he was going to have to do this alone.

Would the man be armed? Tom could only assume so.

He was breathing hard, but his hands had steadied. He had no choice. He had to do this.

Climbing quickly upward, staying behind

the cover of rocks and trees as best he could, Tom topped the hill, keeping low, the gun gripped in both hands.

He knew he couldn't hesitate. Not even an instant. The moment he saw the rustler he would have to shoot. Shoot to kill if the individual was armed. He'd never killed a man. Today could change that.

As Tom Robinson moved through the trees at the edge of a small clearing, he heard a horse whinny off to his left, and spun in that direction, his finger on the trigger.

The moment he saw the animal, and the empty saddle, he realized the mistake he'd made. He spun back around and came face-to-face with the trespasser. Shocked both by who it was and by the tree limb in the man's hands, Tom hesitated an instant too long before pulling the trigger.

The shot boomed among the trees, echoing over the rocks, the misguided bullet burying itself in the bark of a pine off to the trespasser's left.

It happened so fast, Tom didn't even realize he'd fired. He barely felt the blow to his head as the man swung the thick limb like a baseball bat. Instead, Tom just heard a sickening thud as the limb struck his temple, felt his knees give out under him and watched in an odd fascination as the dried needles on the ground came up to meet his face, just before everything went black.

JACKLYN WILDE STARTED at the sound of a knock on the hall door to her motel room. "Delivery."

She sat up in confusion, horrified to realize that she'd dozed off. After the phone call from Stratton, she'd lain down for only a minute, but must have fallen asleep.

She rushed to the receiver terminal, half expecting to see that Dillon was no longer in his room.

But the steady beep assured her he was right next door. Or at least his tracking device was.

She thought about knocking on his door to check, using the food as an excuse. But instead she went to tip the deliveryman, closing her door behind him.

As she placed the Chinese food sacks on the table in the corner of her room, she heard a soft tap on the door between their rooms.

"Dinner's here," she called in response. Unconsciously, she braced herself as he stepped into her room.

His hair was wet and curled at his neck, his face flushed from his bath, and he smelled better than sweet and sour shrimp any day of the week. On top of that, he looked so happy and excited that anyone with a heart would have felt something as he made a beeline for the food.

She knew she was considered cold and heartless with no feelings, especially the female kind. It made it easier in her line of work to let everyone think that.

But how could she not be moved to see Dillon like a kid in a candy store as he opened each of the little white boxes, making delighted sounds and breathing in the scent of each, all the time flashing that grin of his?

"I can't believe this. I think you got all my favorites," he said, turning that grin on her. "You must have read my mind." The look in his eyes softened, taking all the air from the room.

She turned away and pretended to look in her suitcase for something.

"Come on," he said. "Let's eat while it's hot. Work can wait. Can't it?"

She pulled out the map she'd planned to show him later, and glanced toward the small table in the corner and Dillon. "Go ahead and start."

He shook his head. "My mother taught better than that."

Reluctantly, she joined him as he began to dish up the rice. "I just want a little sweet and sour shrimp."

He looked up. "You can't be serious. Who's going to eat all this?"

She couldn't help her smile. "I figured you would. You did say you've been starved for Chinese food."

His grateful expression was almost her undoing—and his subsequent vulnerability as well. He ducked his head as if overcome with emotions he didn't want her to see, and spooned sweet and sour shrimp onto a plate for her.

She made a job of putting the map on the chair beside her, giving him a moment. Maybe she'd underestimated what four years in prison had done to him. Or what it must be like for him to be out.

When she looked up, however, there was no sign of anything on his face except a brilliant smile as he dished up his own plate. She warned herself not to be taken in by any of his antics as she took a bite of her meal and watched him do the same.

He closed his eyes and moaned softly. She tried to ignore him as she pretended to study the map on the chair next to her while she nibbled her food.

"You have to try this."

Before she could react, he reached across the table and shoved a forkful of something at her. Instinctively, she opened her mouth.

"Isn't that amazing?" he asked as he intently watched her chew.

It *was* amazing. Spicy, but not too hot. "Which one is that?" she asked, just to break the tense quiet in the room as he stared at her.

"Orange-peel beef." He was already putting some on her plate. "And wait until you try this." He started toward her with another forkful.

She held up her hand, more than aware of how intimate it was to be fed by a man. She was sure Dillon Savage was aware of it, too. "Really, I—" But the fork had touched her lips and her mouth opened again.

As he dragged the fork away slowly, she felt a rush of heat that had nothing to do with the spicy food.

She met his gaze and felt a chill run the length of her spine. The smile on his lips, the teasing tilt of his head, couldn't hide what was deep in those pale blue eyes.

She had forgotten that she'd been the one to put him behind bars, but clearly, Dillon Savage had not.

Chapter Four

Dillon stared into Jack's gray eyes. For a moment there he'd been enjoying himself, so much that he'd forgotten who she was: the woman who'd sent him to prison. His mood turned sour in an instant.

He dragged his gaze away, but not before she'd seen the change in him. Seen his true feelings.

She shoved her plate aside, her appetite apparently gone, and spread the map out on the table like a barrier between them. "We need to get to work, so as soon as you've finished eating…"

He ate quickly, but his enjoyment of foods he'd missed so much was gone. He told himself it was better this way. Jack had to be aware of how he felt about her. She would have been a fool not to, and this woman was no fool.

But he doubted she knew the extent of his feelings. Or how he'd amused himself those many hours alone in his bunk. He'd plotted his revenge. Not that he planned to act on it, he'd told himself. It had just been something to do. Because he would need to do *something* about the person who'd betrayed him. And while he was at it, why not do something about Jack?

Only he would have to be careful around her. More careful than he'd been so far.

Food forgotten, he shoved the containers aside and stood to lean over the map. But his attention was on Jack. He could tell she was still a little shaken, and wanted to reassure her that he was no longer a man driven by vengeance. No easy task, given that he didn't believe it himself.

But that wasn't what bothered him as he pretended to study the map. As a student of human nature, he couldn't help but wonder why, when he'd been so careful to mask his feelings for years, he had let that mask slip— even for an instant—around the one woman who controlled his freedom.

Jacklyn watched his eyes. They were a pale blue, with tiny specks of gold. Eyes that gave away too much, including the fact that behind all that blue was a brain as sharp as any she'd run across. And that made him dangerous, even beyond whatever grudges he still carried.

On the map, she'd marked with a small red *x* each ranch that had lost cattle. Next to it, she'd put down the number of livestock stolen and the estimated value.

Some of the cattle had been taken in broad daylight, others under the cover of night. The randomness of the hits had made it impossible to catch the rustlers—that and the fact that they worked a two-hundred-mile area, moved fast and left no evidence behind.

Dillon had been leaning over the table, but now sat back and raked a hand through his still-wet hair.

"Something wrong?" she asked. Clearly, there was. She could see that he was upset. If he was the leader of the rustlers, as she suspected, none of this would come as a surprise to him. Unless, of course, his partners in crime had hit more ranches than he was aware of. Had they been cheating him? What if they'd been double-crossing him? She could only hope.

She reminded herself that there was the remote chance Dillon Savage wasn't involved, which meant whoever was leading this band of rustlers was as clever as he had been. Another reason Dillon might have looked upset?

"Just an interesting pattern," he said.

She nodded. She'd been afraid he was going to start lying to her right off the bat. "Interesting how?"

He gave her a look that said she knew as well as he did. "By omission."

"Yes," she agreed, relieved he hadn't tried to con her. "It appears they are saving the biggest ranch for last."

He smiled at that. "You really think they're ever going to stop, when things are going so well for them?"

No. That was her fear. Some of the smaller ranchers were close to going broke. The rustlers had taken a lot of unbranded calves this spring. Based on market value, the animals had been worth about a thousand dollars a head, a loss that was crippling the smaller ranches, some of which had been hit more than once.

Worse, the rustlers were showing no sign of letting up. She'd hoped they would get cocky, mess up, but they were apparently too good for that.

"What do you think?" she asked, motioning to the map.

He leaned back in his chair. "I'm more interested in what you think."

She scowled at him.

"I'm not trying to be difficult," he contended. "I'm just curious as to your take on this. After all, if we're going to be working together…"

She fought the urge to dig in her heels. But he was right. She'd gotten him out of prison to help her catch the rustlers. It was going to require some give and take. But at the same time, if he was the leader…

"I think they're going to make a big hit on Shade Waters's W Bar Ranch. It's the largest spread in the area and the rustlers have already hit ranches around him for miles, but not touched his."

Dillon lifted a brow.

"What?"

"I suspect that's exactly what they want you to think," he said.

She had to bite her tongue. Damn him and his arrogance. "You have a better suggestion as to where they'll go next?"

He leaned forward to study the map again. After a long moment, he said, "Not a clue."

She swore under her breath and glared at him.

"If you're asking me what the rustlers will do next, I have no idea," he said, raising both hands in surrender.

"What would *you* do?" she snapped.

Dillon shrugged, pretty sure now he knew why Jack had gotten him out of prison. "Like I told you back at the prison weeks ago, I'm not sure how I can help you find these guys."

He saw that she didn't believe that. "Look, it's clear that they are very organized. No fly-by-night bunch. They move fast and efficiently. They know what they're doing, where they're going to go next."

"So?" she asked.

"If you think I can predict their movements, then you wasted your time and your money getting me an early release. You might as well drive me back to prison right now."

"Don't tempt me. You said you think they want me to assume they're going to hit Waters's ranch. What does that mean?"

"They wouldn't be that obvious. Sorry, but isn't the reason this bunch has been so hard to catch the fact that they don't do what you expect them to? That gives them the upper hand."

"Tell me something I don't know, Mr. Savage."

He sighed and looked at the map again. "Are these the number of cattle stolen per ranch?" he asked, pointing to the notations she'd made beside the red x's.

She gave him an exasperated look, her jaw still tight.

He could see why she thought the ring would be looking for a big score. The rustlers were being cautious, taking only about fifty head at a time, mostly not-yet-branded calves that would be hard to trace. Smart, but not where the big money was.

Jacklyn got up from the table as if too nervous to sit still, and started clearing up their dinner.

"It's not about the money," he said to her back.

She turned as she tossed an empty Chinese food box into the trash. "Stop trying to con me."

"I'm not. You're looking at this rationally. Rustling isn't always rational—at least the motive behind it isn't. Hell, there are a lot of better ways to make a living."

"I thought you said it was simple math, quick bucks, little risk," she said, an edge to her voice.

So she had been listening. "Yeah, but it's too hit-or-miss. With a real job you get to wear a better wardrobe, have nicer living conditions. Not to mention a 401 K salary, vacation and sick pay, plus hardly anyone ever shoots at you."

"Your point?" she said, obviously not appreciating his sense of humor.

She started to scoop up the map, but he grabbed her hand, more to get her attention than to stop her. He could feel her pulse hammering against the pad of his thumb, which he moved slowly in a circle across the warm flesh. His heart kicked up a beat as her eyes met his.

What the hell was he doing? He let go and she pulled back, her gaze locked with his, a clear warning in all that gunmetal-gray.

"All I'm saying is that you have to think like they think," he said.

She shook her head. "That's *your* job."

"The only way I can do that is if I know what they really want," he said.

"They want *cattle*."

He laughed. "No. Trust me, it's not about cattle. It's always about the end result. The cattle are just a means to an end. What we need to know is what they're getting out of this. It isn't the money. They aren't making enough for it to be about money. So what do they really want?"

"The money will come from a big score. Waters's W Bar Ranch."

"After they've telegraphed what they are going to do so clearly that it's what you're expecting?" He snorted. "No, they have something else in mind."

She shook her head as if he was talking in riddles. "I won't know what they want until I catch them."

He grinned. "Catching them is one thing. Finding out who they are is another."

She was glaring at him again.

"You've been trying to catch an unnamed ring of cattle rustlers," he said patiently. "What do these men do when they aren't rustling cattle? You can bet they work on these ranches," he said, pointing at the map.

She sat back down very slowly. He could tell she was trying to control her temper. She thought he was messing with her.

"Look," he said softly. "You already know a lot about these guys." He ticked items off on his fingers. "One, someone smart is running this operation. That's why these characters seem to know what they're doing and why they haven't made any mistakes. Two, they know the country." He nodded. "We're talking some inside jobs here. They know not only where to find the cattle, but which ones to take and when. They either work on the ranches or have a connection of some kind."

She crossed her arms, scowling but listening.

"Three, they're cowboys. They're too good at working with cattle not to be, and they've used horses for most of their raids. I'll bet you these guys can ride better at midnight on a moonless night in rough terrain than most men can ride in a corral in broad daylight."

She actually smiled at that.

He smiled back, then asked, "What's so humorous?"

"You. You just described yourself," she said, her gaze locking with his. "We're looking for someone just like you. How about that."

WHEN THE CALL CAME hours later, Jacklyn was in the middle of a nightmare. She jerked awake, dragging the bad dream into the room with her as she fumbled for her cell phone beside the bed.

"Tom Robinson's in the hospital," Stratton said without preamble. "He's unconscious. The doctors aren't sure he's going to make it."

Jacklyn fought to wake up, to make sense of what he was saying and what this had to do with her. Although she couldn't remember any specifics of the nightmare, she knew it had been about the leader of the rustling ring. He'd been trying to kill her, stalking her among some trees. She could still feel him out there, feel the danger, the fear, sense him so close that if she looked over her shoulder… It had been Dillon, hadn't it?

"It seems like he might have stumbled across the rustlers," Stratton said. "His hired hand found him near a spot where someone had cut the fence."

She glanced at the clock next to the bed. It was just after midnight.

"Are you there?" Stratton asked irritably. Like her, he'd obviously been awakened by the call about Tom. "When Tom didn't return home for dinner, his hired hand tracked him down, and got him to the hospital. You know what this means, don't you?"

Jacklyn threw off the covers and sat up, trying to throw off the remnants of the dream and the chilling terror that still had her in its grip, too. Snapping on the light beside the bed, she asked, "Did they get any cattle?"

"No. He must have scared the rustlers away."

More awake, she said, "You told everyone to stay out of the area, right? To wait until I got there before they fix the fence?"

"Sheriff McCray already went out to the scene tonight."

She swore under her breath.

"I told Robinson's hired man that you'd be there first thing in the morning. The rustlers have moved up a level on the criminal ladder. If Tom dies, they've gone from rustling to murder." With that he hung up.

She closed her cell phone and, bleary-eyed, glanced again at the clock, then at the monitor. She'd turned it down so there was no steady beep indicating where Dillon Savage was at the moment.

But she could see that he was in the room next door. Probably sleeping like a baby, without a care in the world.

With both a real nightmare and a bad dream hanging over her, she fought the urge to wake him up and ruin his sleep, just as hers had been. She wondered what Dillon Savage's reaction would be to the news.

She turned out the light and crawled back under the covers, even though she doubted she'd get back to sleep. Silently, she prayed that Tom Robinson would regain consciousness and be able to identify his assailants.

The rustlers had messed up this time. They'd been seen. It was their first mistake.

Chapter Five

The drive north the next morning was like going home again for Dillon Savage. Except for the fact that he had no home. Which made seeing the land he knew so well all that much harder to take.

Not to mention that Jack wasn't talking to him. She'd broken the news at breakfast.

"You all right?" he'd finally asked, over pancakes and bacon. She'd seemed angry with him all morning. He couldn't think of anything he'd done recently that would have set her off, but then, given their past...

She'd looked up from her veggie omelet and leveled those icy gray eyes on him. "Tom Robinson was found near death yesterday evening on his ranch. Apparently, he stumbled across the rustlers. He's in the hospital. His ranch hands found him— along with a spot in the fence where the barbed wire had been cut." She'd stared at Dillon, waiting.

"I'm sorry to hear about Tom. I always liked him," he had said, meaning it. But his words only seemed to make Jack's mood more sour, if that was possible.

Tom Robinson was one of the few neighbors who still had his place. Dillon had often wondered how he'd managed to keep his spread when almost all the other ranchers around the W Bar had sold out to Shade Waters.

"If Tom was attacked by the rustlers, then they just went from felony theft to attempted murder," Jack had pointed out. "But the good news is that when Tom regains consciousness, he'll be able to identify them."

"Good," Dillon had said, seeing that she was bluffing. She had no way of knowing if Tom Robinson had gotten a good look at whoever had attacked him, let alone if it was the rustlers. "Sounds like you got a break." She was staring at him, so he frowned at her. *"What?"*

"Come on, Dillon," she'd said, dropping her voice. It was the first time she'd called him by his first name. "You and I both know you're the leader of this rustling ring. Once

Tom identifies who attacked him, your little house of cards is going to come tumbling down. Tell me the truth now and I will try to get you the best deal I can."

He had laughed, shaking his head. "Jack, you're barking up the wrong tree. I'm not your man." He'd grinned and added, "At least not for that role, anyway. I told you. I've gone straight. No more iron bars for me."

She hadn't believed him.

He should have saved his breath, but he'd tried to assure her she was wrong. "There's a lot of injustice in the world. I'm sorry Tom got hurt. But Jack, if you think I have anything to do with this—"

"Don't even bother," she'd snapped, throwing down her napkin. Breakfast was over.

Since then, she hadn't said two words to him.

He stared out his window. The golden prairie was dotted with antelope, geese and cranes, and of course, cows. This was cattle country and had been for two hundred years. Ranch houses were miles apart and towns few and far between.

It amazed Dillon how little things had changed over the years. He kept up on the news and knew that places like Bozeman had been growing like crazy.

But this part of Montana had looked like this for decades, the landscape changing little as the population diminished. Kids left the farms and ranches for greener pastures in real towns or out of state.

But as isolated and unpopulated as this country was, there was a feeling of community. While there had been little traffic this morning, everyone they passed had waved, usually lifting just a couple of fingers from the steering wheel or giving a nod.

There was so much that he'd missed. Some people didn't appreciate this land. It was fairly flat, with only the smudged, purple outline of mountains far in the distance. There was little but prairie, and a pencil-straight, two-lane road running for miles.

But to him it was beautiful. The grasses, a deep green, undulated like waves in the wind. The sky was bluer than any he'd ever seen. Willows had turned a bright gold, dogwood a brilliant red. Everywhere he looked there were birds.

God, how he'd missed this.

He'd known it would be hell coming back

here. Especially after his four-year stint in prison. He'd never dreamed he'd return so soon—or with Jack—let alone have a microchip embedded behind his left ear. Life was just full of surprises.

The farther north Jacklyn drove, the more restless Dillon became. He'd hoped the years in prison had changed him, had at least taught him something about himself. But this place brought it all back. The betrayal. The anger. The aching need for vengeance.

"I'm sorry, where did you say we were going?" he asked. Jack, of course, hadn't said.

"Your old stompin' grounds," she said.

That's what he was afraid of. They'd gone from the motel to pick up a horse trailer, two horses and tack. He couldn't wait to get back in the saddle. He was just worried where that horse was going to take him. Maybe more to the point, what he would do once he and Jack were deep in this isolated country, just the two of them.

JACKLYN HAD HER OWN reasons for not wanting to go north that morning. The big one was that Sheriff Claude McCray had sent word he had to see her.

Claude was the last man she wanted to see. And with good reason. The last time she'd been with him they'd gotten into an argument after making love. She'd broken off their affair, knowing she'd been an idiot to get involved with him in the first place. She was embarrassed and ashamed.

When Dillon had asked her if she didn't regret something she'd done, she'd thought of Sheriff McCray. Since the breakup, she'd made a point of staying out of his part of Montana.

But today she had no choice. And maybe, just maybe, the reason McCray wanted to see her had something to do with Tom Robinson and the men who had attacked him, given the fact that the sheriff had gone to her crime scene last night.

The day was beautiful as she drove out of Lewistown pulling the horse trailer. Behind her, in her rearview mirror, she could see the Big Snowy Mountains and the Little Belts. Once she made it over the Moccasins and the Judiths, the land stretched to the horizon, rolling fields broken only occasionally by rock outcroppings or a lone tree or two.

Jack stared at the straight stick of a road that

ran north, away from the mountains, away from any town of any size, and dreaded seeing Sheriff Claude McCray again—especially with Dillon Savage along.

She'd never forgive herself for foolishly becoming involved with someone she occasionally worked with. Not a good idea. On top of that, she'd gotten involved with Claude for all the wrong reasons.

Jacklyn turned off the two-lane highway onto a narrow, rutted dirt road. As far as the eye could see there wasn't a house or barn. Usually this open land comforted her, but not this morning, with everything she had on her mind. She felt antsy, as if she were waiting for the other shoe to drop.

She'd called the hospital before she'd left the motel. Tom Robinson was in critical condition. It was doubtful he would regain consciousness. She was angry and sickened. She liked Tom.

Selfishly, she'd wanted him to come to in the hopes that he could ID at least one of the rustlers. With just one name, she knew she could put pressure on that individual to identify the person running the ring. Dillon Savage.

She glanced over at him. She'd give him

credit; he'd seemed genuinely upset over hearing about Tom. But was that because he'd known and liked the man, as he'd said? Or because his little gang of rustlers had gone too far this time and now might be found out?

He didn't look too worried that he was going to be caught, she thought. He was slouched in the seat, gazing out the window, watching the world go by as if he didn't have a care. Could she be wrong about him? Maybe. But there *was* something going on with him. She could feel it.

"So we're heading to the Robinson place," Dillon said, guessing that would be at least one of their stops today.

"After that we're going to the W Bar."

He could feel her probing gaze on him again, as if she was waiting for a reaction.

But he wasn't about to give her one. He just nodded, determined not to let her see how he felt about even the thought of crossing Shade Waters's path. He hadn't seen Waters since the day Jack had arrested him.

The truth was she'd probably saved his life, given that Shade had had a shotgun—and every intention of killing Dillon on the spot that day.

"Waters know you got me out of prison?" he asked.

"Probably the reason he wants to see me."

Dillon chuckled. "This should be interesting then."

"You'll be staying in the pickup—and out of trouble. Your work with me has nothing to do with Shade Waters," she said in that crisp, no-nonsense tone.

He smiled. "Just so I'm there to witness his reaction when you tell him that. Unless you want to leave me at the bar in Hilger and pick me up on your way back."

She shot him a look. "Until this rustling ring is caught, you and I are attached at the hip."

"I do like that image," he said, and grinned over at her.

She scowled and went back to her driving. "Any animosity you have for Waters or any other ranchers, you're to keep to yourself."

"What animosity?" he asked with a straight face. "I'm a changed man. Any hard feelings I had about Shade Waters I left behind that razor wire fence you broke me out of."

She gave him a look that said she'd believe that when hell froze over. "Just remember what I said. I don't need any trouble out of you. I have enough with Waters."

"Don't worry, Jack, I'll be good," Dillon said, and pulled down the brim on his hat as he slid down in the seat again. He tried not to think about Tom Robinson or Shade Waters or even Jack.

Instead, he thought about lying in the bathtub last night at the motel, bubbles up to his neck. And later, sprawled on the big bed, staring up at the ceiling, trying to convince himself he wasn't going to blow his freedom. Not for anything. Even justice.

The bath had been pure heaven. The bed was huge and softer than anything he'd slept on in years. In prison, he'd had a pad spread on a concrete slab. A real bed had felt strange, and had made him wonder how long it would take to get used to being out.

How long did it take not to be angry that normal no longer felt normal? Maybe as long as getting over the fact that someone owed him for the past four years of his life.

SHERIFF CLAUDE MCCRAY wasn't in, but the dispatcher said she was expecting him, and to wait in his office.

Ten minutes later, Claude walked in. He was a big man, powerfully built, with a chiseled face and deep-set brown eyes. He gave Jacklyn a look that could have wilted lettuce. His gaze turned even more hostile when he glanced at Dillon.

McCray chuckled to himself as he moved behind his desk, shaking his head as he glared at Jacklyn again. "Dillon Savage. You got the bastard out. What a surprise."

She met his eyes for only an instant before she looked away, not wanting to get into this with him. Especially in front of Dillon, given what Claude had accused her of nearly four years ago.

"You're obsessed with Dillon Savage," McCray had said.

"Excuse me? It's my job to find him and stop him," she'd snapped back.

"Oh, Jacklyn, it's way beyond that. You admire him, admit it."

"Wh-what?" she'd stammered, sliding out of bed, wanting to distance herself from this ridiculous talk.

"He's the only one who's ever eluded you this long," Claude had called after her. *"You're making a damn hero out of him."*

She had been barely able to speak, she was so shocked. "That's so ridiculous, I don't even— You're jealous of a cattle rustler?"

He'd narrowed his eyes at her angrily. "I'm jealous of a man you can't go five minutes without talking about."

"I'm sorry I bothered you with talk about my job," she'd snapped as she jerked on her jeans and boots and looked around for her bra and sweater.

Claude was sitting up in the bed, watching her, frowning. "I'd bet you spend more time thinking about Dillon Savage than you do me."

She'd heard the jealousy and bitterness in his voice and had been sickened by it. He'd called her after that, telling her he'd had too much to drink and didn't know what he was saying.

For all his apologies, that had been the end of their affair. She'd caught Dillon a few days later and had made a point of staying as far from Sheriff Claude McCray as possible, even though he'd tried to contact her repeatedly over the past four years.

Now, as Claude settled into his chair behind the large metal desk, she noticed that he looked shorter than she remembered, his shoulders less broad. Or maybe she couldn't help comparing him to Dillon Savage. They were both close to the same age, but that was where the similarities ended.

"What's the world coming to when we have to get criminals out of prison to help solve crimes?" McCray said as if to himself, looking from Dillon to Jack.

"Is there anything new on the Robinson case?" she asked, determined to keep the conversation on track.

"Why don't you ask your boyfriend here," McCray quipped.

Dillon was watching this interplay with interest. She swore under her breath, wishing that she'd come alone. But she didn't like letting Dillon out of her sight. Especially now that the stakes were higher, with Tom Robinson critical.

"Sheriff, I just need to know if you have any leads. I understand you went out to the crime scene last night." She had to bite her tongue to keep from saying how stupid it was to go out there in the dark and possibly destroy evidence. "I'm headed out there now."

"Don't waste your time. There's nothing to find."

She would be the judge of that. "What about the Drummond place?"

Claude was shaking his head. "Wasn't worth riding back in there for so few head of cattle."

Bud Drummond might argue that, she thought.

She rose from her chair, anxious to get out of Claude's office. She'd thought about not even bothering to come here, but he'd sent word that he wanted to see her. She should have known it wasn't about the Robinson case.

Her real reason for coming, she knew, was so he wouldn't think she was afraid to face him. Perish the thought.

"If Tom Robinson dies, it will be murder," McCray said, glaring at Dillon. "This time you'll stay in prison."

Dillon, to his credit, didn't react. But she could see that this situation could escalate easily if they didn't leave. Claude seemed to be working himself up for a fight.

"We're going," Jacklyn said, moving toward the door.

The sheriff rose, coming around the desk to grab her arm. "I need to speak with you alone."

Jacklyn looked down at his fingers digging

into her flesh. He let go of her, but she saw Dillon leap to his feet, about to come to her defense.

That was the last thing she needed. "Mr. Savage, if you wouldn't mind waiting by the pickup..." She had no desire to be alone with Claude McCray, but if she was anything, she was no coward. And he just might have something to tell her about the investigation that Dillon shouldn't hear.

Dillon frowned, as if he didn't like leaving her alone with McCray. Obviously, she wasn't the only one who thought the man could be dangerous.

She indicated the door and gave Dillon an imploring look.

"I'll be right outside if you need me," he said as he opened the door and stepped out, closing it quietly behind him.

"That son of a bitch." The sheriff swore and swung on her. "He acts like he owns you. Are you already sleeping with him?"

"Don't be ridiculous. What was it you had to say to me?"

He glared at her, anger blazing in his eyes. "If you're not, it's just a matter of time before you are. You've had something for him for years."

"If that's all you wanted to say…" She started for the door.

He reached to grab her again, but this time she avoided his grasp. "Don't," she said, her voice low and full of warning. "Don't touch me."

He drew back in surprise. "Jackie—"

"And don't call me that."

He stiffened and busied himself straightening his hat, as if trying to get his temper under control.

What had she ever seen in him? She didn't want to think about why she'd ended up with McCray. And it wasn't because she hadn't known what kind of man he was. She'd been looking for an outlaw during the day and had wanted one at night, as well.

Too late she'd realized Claude McCray was a mean bastard with even less ethics than Dillon Savage.

"Was there something about the case?" she asked as she reached for the doorknob.

He glared at her for a long moment, then grudgingly said, "My men found something up by where the rustlers cut the barbed wire of Robinson's fence last night," he said finally. "I'm sure it's probably been in the dirt for years and has nothing do with the rustlers, but

I was told to give it to you." He reached toward his desk, then turned and dropped a gold good-luck piece into her palm.

"You have any idea who this might belong to?" she asked.

"Someone whose luck is about to turn for the worst," McCray said cryptically. "At least if I have anything to do with it."

Chapter Six

"You all right?" Dillon asked as Jack came out of the sheriff's office.

"Fine," she said, whipping past him and heading for the truck.

He followed, thinking about what he'd seen in there. Definitely tension between the lawman and Jack. Dillon had never liked that redneck son of a bitch, McCray. He'd seen plenty of guys like him at prison. What he'd witnessed in the office hadn't made Dillon dislike him any less.

In fact, it had been all he could do not to punch the man. But if Dillon had learned anything it was that you didn't punch out a sheriff. Especially when you had just gotten a prerelease from prison and were treading on thin ice as it was.

Jack started the pickup as Dillon slid in and

slammed the door. She seemed anxious to get out of town. He knew that feeling.

"So what did the bastard do to you?"

She jerked her head around to look at him and almost ran into the car in front of them.

He saw the answer in her expression and swore. "McCray. Oh man." Dillon had hoped the animosity between them just had to do with work, but he'd known better. He just hadn't wanted to believe she'd get involved with Claude McCray, and said as much.

"Don't," she warned as she gripped the wheel. The light changed and she got the pickup going again. "You and I aren't getting into this discussion."

He shook his head. "I've made some big mistakes in my life, but Claude McCray?"

She slammed on the brakes so hard the seat belt cut into him. "I will not have this discussion with you," she said, biting off each word. The driver behind them laid on his horn. Jack didn't seem to notice. She was clasping the wheel so tightly her knuckles were white, her eyes straight ahead, as if she couldn't look at him.

"Okay, okay," Dillon said, realizing this

had to be that big regret he'd sensed in her. Jack's big mistake.

It was so unlike her. She had more sense than to get involved with McCray. Something must have caused it. "When was it?"

"I just said—"

He swore as he remembered something he'd overheard while in the county jail. "You were seeing him when you were chasing me."

She groaned and got the pickup going again. "Could we please drop this? Can't you just sit over there and laugh smugly under your breath so I don't have to hear it?"

She still hadn't looked at him.

He reached over and touched her arm. Her gaze shifted to him slowly, reluctantly. He looked into her eyes and saw a pain he couldn't comprehend. No way had McCray broken it off between them. No, from the way the sheriff had been acting, Jack had dumped *him*.

So what was with this heartache Dillon saw in her eyes?

TOM ROBINSON'S RANCH house was at the end of a narrow, deeply rutted road. The ranch was small, a wedge of land caught between Waters's huge spread and Reda Harper's much less extensive one.

The ride north had been pure hell. Though Dillon finally shut up about her and Sheriff McCray, Jack knew he was sitting over there making sport of her entire affair. She hated to think what was going through his mind.

After a few miles, she stole a glance at him. He had his hat down over his eyes, his long legs sprawled out, his hands resting in his lap. To all appearances, he seemed to be sleeping.

Right. He was over there chortling to himself, pleased that he'd stirred her up again. Worse, that he now had something on her. The man was impossible.

She would never figure him out. Earlier, when he'd forced her to look at him, she'd thought she'd seen compassion in his eyes, maybe even understanding.

But how could he understand? She didn't herself.

Dillon Savage was like no man she'd ever known. When she'd been chasing him before, she'd been shocked to learn that he didn't fit any profile, let alone that of a cattle rustler. For starters, he was university educated, with degrees in engineering, business and psychology, and he'd graduated at the top of his class.

If that wasn't enough, he'd inherited a bundle right before he started rustling cattle. He had no reason to commit the crime. Except, she suspected, to flaunt the law.

Dillon stirred as she pulled into Tom Robinson's yard. She felt the gold good-luck coin in her pocket. She'd almost forgotten that she'd stuck it there, she'd been so upset about McCray—and Dillon.

She knew it might not be a clue. Anyone could have dropped it there at any time. While the coin did look old, that didn't mean it was. Nor would she put it past Claude McCray to lie about where he'd found it, just to throw her off track. Worse, she suspected it might be fairly common, even something given out by casinos, since Montana had legalized gambling.

If it had belonged to one of the rustlers, any fingerprints on it had been destroyed with McCray handling it.

She sighed and reached into her pocket for the coin, thinking about what McCray had said about luck changing for the person who'd been carrying it.

"I need to ask you something," she said, turning to Dillon. "I need you to tell me the truth."

He nodded and grinned. "Did I tell you I never lie?"

"Right."

Dillon looked at the hand she held toward him, her fingers clasped around something he couldn't see, her eyes intent on his face.

He felt his stomach clench as she slowly uncurled her fingers. He had no idea what she was going to show him. And even though he suspected it wasn't going to be good, he wasn't prepared for what he saw nestled in her palm.

"You recognize it!" she accused, wrapping her fingers back around it as if she wanted to hit him with her fist. "So help me, if you deny it—"

"Yeah, I've seen it before. Or at least one like it."

She was staring at him as if she was surprised he'd actually admitted it. "Who does it belong to?"

"I said I'd seen one like it, I didn't say—"

"Don't," she snapped, scowling at him.

"Easy," he said, holding up his hands. "A friend of mine used to have one like it, okay? He carried it around for luck. But he's dead."

"And you don't know what happened to his?"

Dillon couldn't very well miss her sarcasm. "May I look at it?"

She reluctantly opened her hand, as if she thought he might grab it and run.

He plucked the good-luck coin from her warm palm, accidentally brushing his fingertips across her skin, and saw her shudder. But his attention was on the coin as he turned it in his fingers. The small marks were right where he knew they would be, leaving no doubt. His heart began to pound.

"Where did you say you got this?" he asked as he handed it back.

Her gaze burned into him. "I didn't."

Dillon could only assume that, since she'd gone to the sheriff about Tom Robinson, McCray had given it to her. Which had to mean that she suspected one of the rustlers who'd attacked Tom had dropped it.

"So who was the deceased friend of yours who had one like it?" she asked, clearly not believing him.

"Halsey Waters. And as for what happened to his coin," Dillon said, "I personally put it in his suit pocket at his funeral."

"Halsey *Waters?* Shade's oldest son?"

"That's the one." Out of the corner of his

eye, Dillon saw the ranch house door open and a stocky cowboy step out. Arlen Dubois.

It was turning out to be like old home week, Dillon thought. All the old gang was back in central Montana. Just as they had been for Halsey Waters's funeral.

ARLEN DUBOIS WAS all cowboy, long and lanky, legs bowed, boots run-down, jeans worn and dirty. He invited them into the house, explaining that he was looking after everything with Tom in the hospital.

Jacklyn watched Arlen take off his hat and nervously rake a hand through short blond curls. His skin was white and lightly freckled where the hat had protected it from the sun. The rest of his face was sunburned red.

He looked from Jacklyn to Dillon and quickly back again. "I'd offer you something to drink…"

"We're fine," Jacklyn said, noticing how uncomfortable the cowboy was in the presence of his old friend. Arlen had a slight lisp, buckteeth and a broad open face. "I just want to ask you a few questions."

He shifted on his feet. "Okay."

"Do you mind if we sit down?" she asked.

Arlen got all flustered, but waved them toward chairs in the small living room. Jacklyn noticed that the fabric was threadbare, and doubted the furnishings had been replaced in Tom's lifetime.

Arlen turned his hat in his hands as he sat on the edge of one of the chairs.

"You work for Tom Robinson?" she asked.

"Yep, but you already know that. If you think I had anything to do with what happened to Tom—"

"How long have you worked for Mr. Robinson?"

Arlen gave that some thought, scraping at a dirty spot on his hat as he did. "About four years," he said, without looking up. The same amount of time Dillon Savage had been behind bars.

"You and Mr. Savage here have been friends for a long time, right?"

Arlen started. "What does that have to do with this? If you think I ever stole cattle with him—"

"I was just asking if you were friends."

Arlen shrugged, avoiding Dillon's gaze. "We knew each other."

Yeah, she would just bet. She'd long suspected Dillon hadn't done the rustling alone.

He would have needed help. But would he have involved a man like Arlen Dubois? Word at the bar was that Dubois tended to brag when he had a few drinks in him, although few people believed even half of what he said.

"Have you seen anyone suspicious around the ranch? Before Tom was attacked?" she asked, knowing that most of her questions were a waste of time. She had just wanted to see Arlen and Dillon together.

Dillon seemed cool as a cucumber, like a man who had nothing to hide.

"Nothin' suspicious," Arlen said, with a shake of his head.

"You know of anyone who had a grudge against Tom?"

The cowboy shook his head again. "Tom was likable enough."

Dillon was studying Arlen, and making him even more nervous. Maybe she should have left him in the truck.

"If you think of anything…"

Arlen looked relieved. "Sure," he said, and rose from his chair. "You ready to ride out to where I found Tom?"

Jacklyn nodded. "One more thing," she said as she stood and reached into her pocket. "Ever seen this before?"

Arlen reacted as if she'd held out a rattlesnake. His gaze shot to Dillon's, then back to the coin. "I might have seen one like it once."

"Where was that?" she asked.

"I can't really recall."

Both of Arlen's responses were lies.

"Mr. Savage, would you mind waiting for me in the pickup?" she asked.

"Not at all, Ms. Wilde."

She ground her teeth as she waited for him to close the front door behind him. "Anything you want to tell me, Arlen?"

"About what?" he asked, looking scared.

"Did you happen to be at Halsey Waters's funeral?"

All the color left his face. "What does that have to do with—"

"Yes or no? Or can't you remember that, either?"

He had the good grace to flush. "I was there, just like all his other friends."

She detected something odd in his tone. Today was the first time she'd heard anything about Halsey Waters. But then, she wasn't from this part of Montana. "How did Halsey die?"

Arlen looked down at his boots. "He was bucked off a wild horse. Broke his neck."

ALL THE OLD DEMONS that had haunted him came back with a vengeance as Dillon rode out with Arlen and Jacklyn, across rolling hills dotted with cattle and sagebrush. He breathed in the familiar scents as if to punish himself. Or remind himself that even four years in prison couldn't change a man enough to forget his first love. Or his worst enemy.

The air smelled so good it made him ache. This had once been his country. He knew it even better than the man who owned it.

They followed the fence line as it twisted alongside the creek, the bottomlands thick with chokecherry, willow and dogwood. Jacklyn slowed her horse, waiting for him.

The memories were so sharp and painful he had to look away for fear she would see that this was killing him.

Or worse, that she might glimpse the desire for vengeance burning in his eyes.

"I've always wanted to ask you," she said conversationally. Arlen was riding ahead of them, out of earshot. "Why three university degrees?"

Dillon pretended to give her question some thought, although he doubted that's what she'd been thinking about. She'd made it clear back at the ranch house that she thought he and Arlen used to rustle cattle together. It hadn't helped that Arlen had lied through his teeth about the good-luck coin.

Shoving back his hat, Dillon shrugged and said, "I was a rancher's son. You know how, at that age, you're so full of yourself. I thought the last thing I wanted to do was ranch. I wanted a job where I got to wear something other than jeans and boots, have an office with a window, make lots of money."

She glanced over at him, as if wondering if he was serious. "You know, I suspect you often tell people what you think they want to hear."

He laughed and shook his head. "Nope, that's the real reason I got three degrees. I was covering my bets."

She cut her eyes to him as she rode alongside him, their legs almost touching. "Okay, I get the engineering and business degrees. But psychology?"

He wondered what she was really asking. "I'm fascinated by people and what makes them tick. Like you," he said, smiling at her. "You're a mystery to me."

"Let's not go there."

"What if I can't help myself?"

"Mr. Savage—"

He laughed. "Maybe before this is over I'll get a glimpse of the real Jack Wilde," he said, her gaze heating him more than the sun beating down from overhead.

He could see that she wished she hadn't started this conversation when she urged her horse forward, trotting off after Arlen Dubois.

As Dillon stared after her retreating backside, he suspected he and the real Jacklyn Wilde were more alike than she ever wanted to admit—and he said as much when he caught up to her.

JACKLYN PRETENDED NOT TO hear him. His voice had dropped to a low murmur that felt like a whisper across her skin. It vibrated in her chest, making her nipples tighten and warmth rush through her, straight to her center.

Dillon chuckled, as if suspecting only too well what his words did to her.

She cursed her foolishness. She should have known better than to try to egg Dillon

Savage on. He was much better at playing head games than she was.

In front of her, Arlen brought his horse up short. She did the same when she noticed the cut barbed wire fence. Dismounting, she handed the cowboy her reins and walked across the soft earth toward the gap.

There was one set of horseshoe tracks in the dirt on the other side of the cut fence, a half-dozen on this side, obliterating Tom's horse's prints. Sheriff McCray and his men. She could see where they had ridden all over, trampling any evidence.

But she no longer thought McCray had planted the lucky gold coin. Not after both Dillon's and Arlen's reactions. She just didn't know what a coin belonging to the deceased Halsey Waters had to do with this ring of rustlers. But she suspected Dillon and Arlen did.

Bending down, she noted that there was nothing unique about the trespasser's horse's prints. She could see where Tom had followed the man toward the creek bottom.

Arlen Dubois had tracked Tom and found him. At least that was the cowboy's story. Unfortunately, McCray and his men had destroyed any evidence to prove it.

She swung back into her saddle. "Show me where you found Tom," she said to Arlen. Turning, she looked back at Dillon. He seemed lost in thought, frowning down at the cut barbed wire.

"Something troubling you?" she asked him.

He seemed to come out of his daze, putting a smile on his face to cover whatever had been bothering him. If he was the leader of the rustlers, then wouldn't he feel something for a man who might die because of him and his partners in crime?

She followed the trampled tracks in the dust, feeling the hot sun overhead. It wasn't until she reached the trees and started up the hillside that she turned, and wasn't surprised to see Arlen and Dillon sitting astride their horses, engaged in what appeared to be a very serious conversation below her.

At the top of the ridge, she found blood-stained earth and scuffed tracks—dozens of boot prints. There was no way to distinguish the trespasser's. Had that been Sheriff McCray's intent? To destroy the evidence? Her one chance to maybe find out who the rustlers were? McCray would do it out of spite.

But there was another explanation, she

realized. McCray might be covering for someone. Or even involved…

She couldn't imagine any reason Claude McCray would get involved in rustling. But then, she wasn't the best judge of character when it came to men, she admitted as she looked down the slope to where Dillon and Arlen were waiting.

By circling the area, she found the trespasser's tracks, and followed them to where he'd made a second cut in the barbed wire to let himself and his horse onto state grazing land.

Then she headed back to where she'd left the two men. As she approached, she noticed that Dillon had ridden over to a lone tree and was lounging under it, chewing on a piece of dried grass, his long legs stretched out and crossed at the ankles, his hat tilted down, but his eyes on her. He couldn't have looked more relaxed. Or more sexy. She couldn't help but wonder what he'd been talking about with Arlen.

Back at the ranch, she let Dillon unsaddle their horses while she went out to the barn, where Arlen was putting his own horse and tack away. He seemed surprised to see her, obviously hoping that she'd already left.

"Thanks for your help today," she said, wondering what he would do for a job if Tom Robinson didn't make it. "Looks like you could use a new pair of boots."

Arlen looked down in surprise. "These are my lucky boots," he said bashfully. He lifted one leg to touch the worn leather, and Jack saw how the sole was worn evenly across the bottom.

Lucky boots. Good-luck coin. Cowboys were a superstitious bunch. "You'll be walking on your socks pretty soon," she said. "I saw you talking to Dillon. Mind telling me what you two were chatting about?"

Arlen gave a lazy shrug. "Nothin' in particular. Just talking about prison and Tom and—" he dropped his gaze "—you. Don't mean to tell you your business, but if I were you, I'd be real careful around him. When he's smiling is when he's the most dangerous."

DILLON WATCHED JACK COME out of the barn, and knew Arlen had said something to upset her.

Dillon had loaded the horses into the trailer and was leaning against the side, waiting for her in the shade. He hadn't been able to get Halsey's good-luck coin off his mind.

"Get what you needed?" he asked as Jack walked past him to climb behind the wheel.

He opened his door and slid in.

"I saw you and Arlen talking. Looked pretty serious," she said, without reaching to start the truck.

"Think we were plotting something?" He laughed.

"You said yourself that the rustlers might work for the ranchers they were stealing cattle from."

Dillon let out a snort. "Arlen? That cowboy can't keep his mouth shut. If he was riding with the gang, you'd have already caught them. The guy is a dim bulb."

Maybe. Or maybe that's what Dillon wanted her to believe. She looked back at Arlen. He was standing in the shade of the barn, watching them.

Dillon sighed. "I was asking him what he was going to do now. He said even if Tom regains consciousness, his injuries are such that he won't be running the ranch anymore. Waters has offered Arlen a job."

"What's wrong with that?" Jacklyn asked, as she heard Dillon curse under his breath.

"Arlen? He's worthless. Tom just kept him on because no one else would hire him. The only reason Waters would make the offer is so Arlen keeps him informed on everything that's going on with Tom and the ranch." At her confused look, Dillon added, "Waters has been trying to buy the Robinson ranch for years."

"Tom is in no condition to sell his ranch—"

"Tom has a niece back East, his only living relative. In his will, apparently he set it up so if anything happened to him and he couldn't run the place or he died…."

"You think she'll sell to Shade Waters."

"Waters will make sure she does."

Jacklyn could understand how Shade might want Tom Robinson's ranch. With it, he would own all the way to the Missouri on this side of the Judith River. The Robinson spread had been the only thing standing in his way.

Chapter Seven

Jacklyn followed the county road as it wound around one section of land after another, until she saw the sign that marked the various directions to ranches in the area.

At one time there'd been a dozen signs tacked on the wooden post. But over the years, most ranches had been bought out, all of them by Shade Waters.

Now there were only three signs on the post, pointing to Shade Waters's W Bar Ranch, Tom Robinson's ranch and Reda Harper's RH Circle Cross.

Jacklyn saw Dillon glance at the signs, his gaze hardening before it veered away. Not far up the road, she turned to drive under an arched entry with W Bar Ranch carved into the graying wood.

"I'll stay in the pickup," he said as she pulled up in the ranch yard.

She looked at him, then at the sprawling ranch house. Shade Walters had come out onto the porch. Always a big man, he wasn't quite as handsome as he'd been in his younger days, but he was still striking. He stood in the shadow of the porch roof, an imposing figure that demanded attention.

The front door opened again and his son Nate came out, letting the door slam behind him. She saw Shade's irritated expression and the way he scowled in Nate's direction.

Nate was in his early thirties, big boned and blond. Unlike his father, his western clothing was new and obviously expensive. Shade Waters looked like every working rancher she'd known, from his worn western shirt to his faded jeans and weathered boots.

She couldn't help but think that whoever had attacked Tom Robinson had come by way of the W Bar, Shade Waters's land.

Nate was staring toward her passenger, and it dawned on her that Dillon and he were close in age and must have gone to school together. The old Savage place had been up the road. Had they once been friends, as had Dillon and Nate's brother, Halsey?

Nate's frown and the intense silence coming from the man next to her made it clear that the two were no longer friends, whatever their relationship had been in the past.

"You won't get out of the pickup no matter what happens?" she asked quietly, without looking at Dillon.

"Nope."

As Jacklyn started to open her door, a pretty, dark-haired woman joined the two men on the porch. Jacklyn felt Dillon tense beside her. The woman looped her arm through Nate's and gazed out at the pickup, as if daring anyone to try to stop her—including Shade Waters. Judging from his expression, he wasn't happy to see the woman join him, any more than he had been his son.

But it was Dillon's reaction that made Jacklyn hesitate before she climbed out of the truck.

Dillon knew the woman. Not just knew her. His left hand was clenched in a fist and his jaw was tight with anger.

She knew he blamed Shade Waters for what had happened not just to his family ranch but to his father. But was there more to the story? Was there a woman involved?

This dark-haired beauty?

"Holler if you need me," Dillon said as she started to climb out of the truck.

She shot him a look as he drew the brim of his hat down over his eyes and leaned back as if planning to sleep until she returned.

Right. As if he wouldn't be watching and listening to everything that was said. She noticed that he'd managed to power down his window before she turned off the pickup engine.

"Enjoy your nap," she said, knowing he wouldn't.

His lips tipped up in a smile. He wasn't fooling her and he knew it.

As Jacklyn closed the truck door, she noticed that the woman had her own gaze fixed on the passenger side of the pickup. On Dillon.

Jacklyn knew there'd been women in Dillon's life. Probably a lot of them. Had he turned to crime because of one of them? Maybe this one?

Jacklyn approached the porch slowly, afraid all hell was about to break loose. She just hoped Dillon Savage wasn't going to be in the middle of it.

MORGAN LANDERS. Dillon couldn't believe his eyes. He'd heard she'd gone to California. Or Florida. That she'd snagged some old guy with lots of bucks.

But as he watched her lean intimately into Nate Waters, Dillon knew he shouldn't have been surprised that Morgan had come back— or why.

What did surprise him was his reaction to seeing her. He hadn't expected ever to lay eyes on her again. Especially not here. It felt like another betrayal, but then he suspected it wasn't her first. Or her last.

What bothered him was that he knew Jack had seen his reaction. She missed little. Now she would think he still felt something for Morgan.

From under his hat, he watched Jack walk to the bottom step of the porch. Clearly, Shade Waters wasn't going to invite her inside the house. Manners had never been the man's strong suit. No, Waters wanted to intimidate her. How better than to stand on the porch, literally looking down on her?

Dillon smiled to himself. He'd put his money on Jack anyday, though. Not even Shade Waters could intimidate a woman like Jacklyn Wilde.

The rancher glanced at the pickup, no doubt seeing that Dillon had has side window down. Another reason Waters wouldn't invite Jack inside. He'd want Dillon to hear whatever he had to say. And Dillon was sure Waters had a lot to say, given that he'd demanded Jack stop by to see him.

Also, Dillon thought with a grin, Waters wouldn't want to go in the house knowing that a Savage was on his property, alone. Waters would be afraid of what Dillon might do.

As Dillon shifted his gaze from Morgan Landers to the elderly man he'd spent years hating, he thought Waters was wise to worry.

JACKLYN LOOKED UP at the three standing on the porch. They made no move to step aside so she could enter the house—or even join them in the shade.

"I can handle this," Shade said, scowling over at his son. But Nate didn't move. Nor did the woman beside him.

Jacklyn couldn't help being curious about the woman, given that Dillon obviously had some connection to her. "I don't believe we've met," she said. "I'm Jacklyn Wilde."

The brunette had the kind of face and body that could stop traffic, but that had nothing to do with the dislike Jacklyn had felt for her instantly.

"Morgan Landers." She flicked her gaze over Jacklyn dismissively, her brown eyes lighting again on the pickup and no doubt the passenger sitting in it.

"If we're through with introductions…" Shade Waters snapped.

Jacklyn waited. She could see how agitated the rancher was, but wasn't entirely certain it had anything to do with her.

"Do you people have any idea what you're doing?" he finally demanded, tilting his head toward the pickup and Dillon.

"You want the rustlers caught?" she asked, resenting him trying to tell her how to do her job.

Waters smirked. "The rustler was *already* behind bars. That is, until you got him out. What the hell were you thinking?"

"Dillon Savage is my problem."

"You're right about that," the big man said angrily. "You going to try to tell me he doesn't know anything about what's been going on?"

She wasn't. Nor was she about to admit that she suspected the same thing he did when it came to Dillon Savage.

"It's his boys who are stealing all the cattle," Waters said with a curse. "That bunch he used to run around with. He's been orchestrating the whole thing from prison, and now you go and get him out so he can lead you in circles. You don't really think he's going to help you catch them, do you?"

"What bunch are we talking about?" she asked, ignoring the rest of what he'd said.

"Buford Cole, Pete Barclay, Arlen Dubois—that bunch," Waters snapped.

"What makes you think it's them? Or are you just making unfounded accusations? Because if you have some evidence—"

Waters let out another curse. "Hell, if I had evidence I'd take it to Sheriff McCray and the rustlers would be behind bars. Everyone in the county knows that Buford Cole and Arlen Dubois were riding with Savage before he went to prison."

"There was never any evidence—"

"Don't give me that evidence bull," Waters snapped. "Just because you couldn't prove it."

"I'm confused. Arlen Dubois just told me you offered him a job. If you really believe he's one of the rustlers…"

Waters's smile never reached his eyes. "Sometimes it's better to have the fox living in the henhouse so you can keep an eye on him. That's one reason I hired Pete Barclay. He also used to run with Savage."

That was also never proved, but she decided not to argue the point. "What about Buford Cole?"

"He's working at the stockyard," Waters stated, and raised a brow as if that said everything.

She looked at Nate. "Didn't you used to run with those same cowboys?"

Nate appeared surprised that she'd said anything to him. "What?"

"I heard you were all friends, including Dillon and your brother, Halsey."

The older Waters's face blanched and he looked as if he might suddenly grab his chest and keel over.

"Now just a minute," Nate said.

"What the hell are you trying to do?" Waters interrupted, taking a step toward her. "Don't you ever bring up Halsey's name in the same breath as those others!"

She noticed he was fine with Nate's name being mentioned with the others. Nate had noticed it, too, and was scowling in his father's direction.

"I'm just saying that because this group used to be friends, there is no evidence they are now involved in rustling cattle together."

Her gaze went to Morgan Landers. She was smiling as if enjoying this.

"The damn rustlers are closing in on my ranch. Even you should be able to see that." Waters's face was now flushed, his voice breaking with emotion. "I can't protect my land or my livestock, not even if I hire a hundred men. Not when half of the range is badlands and only accessible by horseback."

She wanted to point out that the rustlers would have the same problem. But Waters was right. Huge sections of his land were inaccessible except by horseback, and given the size of the place, it would take several days to ride across the length of the W Bar. No amount of men could protect it completely.

"Your ranch hasn't been hit by the rustlers," she pointed out. "Do you have some reason to believe it will be?"

Waters looked flustered, something she didn't think happened often. "They must know I'll shoot to kill if they try to take my cattle."

"I wouldn't advise that," Jacklyn said.

"Then what are you going to do to stop them?" he demanded.

"I'm going to catch them, but I'll need your help. Tell me where your cattle are, what precautions you've taken and what men you have available to guard the key borders."

Waters looked at her, then glanced toward the pickup and laughed. "You don't really think I'm going to give you that information, do you? Why don't I just run it in the newspaper so the rustlers know exactly when and where to steal my cattle?"

"If this is about Mr. Savage—"

"You can try to explain until you're blue in the face why you got Dillon Savage out of prison, young woman, but I'm not giving you a damn thing. I'll take care of my stock as best I can. Just know I'll do whatever I have to, and that includes killing the sons of bitches." He was looking toward the truck again. "I have the right to protect my property."

"Mr. Waters—"

"I don't have time for this," he said, and thumped down the steps and past her, headed toward the barn.

"Like we're going to hold our breaths and wait for you to catch the rustlers," his son muttered.

"Shut up, Nate," Waters snapped over his shoulder.

"Mr. Waters," Jacklyn said, trailing after him. "I want your permission to put some video devices on your ranch. If you're right, the rustlers have probably been watching your operation already."

"No," he said, without stopping or looking back. "I told you I was going to take care of things my own way."

"If your own way is illegal—"

He swung around so fast she almost ran into him. "Listen, maybe you will catch the rustlers. But it won't be on my ranch. I won't be spied on."

"Spied on?"

"Videos and all that paraphernalia. No. Maybe that's the way it's done nowadays, but I don't want a bunch of your people on my land, and I know for a fact you can't force them on me."

Jacklyn glanced back at the truck. She couldn't see Dillon's face through the sunlight glinting off the windshield, but she knew he hadn't missed a thing.

Then she followed Shade Waters into the barn, determined to do her job despite him.

DILLON WATCHED MORGAN give him a backward glance before she followed Nate Waters into the house. She'd stared in his direction, as if she'd been expecting to see him.

Unlike him, who hadn't been prepared to see her again ever. As the front door closed, he sat without moving, bombarded by memories of the two of them.

Morgan. There'd been a time when she'd made him think about buying another ranch and settling down. But even Morgan couldn't still the quiet rage inside him. Not that Morgan had wanted him to be anything but a rustler. She liked the drama. She'd never wanted him to quit rustling.

She was hooked on the danger, never knowing when he would sneak into town and into her bed, never knowing if her house would be raided by the sheriff's men.

And since Morgan had no way of knowing about Dillon's inheritance, she'd just assumed he would never have enough money to keep her in the way she wanted to live, so she'd never even mentioned marriage. And he'd never told her different.

He wondered idly if she was serious about Nate Waters. Or if she was only serious about his money. Morgan would like the power that came with the Waters name, as well.

As Jacklyn disappeared into the barn with the rancher, Dillon fought the turmoil he felt inside. Seeing Morgan had brought back the past in a blinding flash. All his good intentions not to let what had happened drag him back into trouble again seemed to fly out the window. He felt the full power of the old bitterness, the resentment, the injustice that burned like hot oil inside him.

Worse, while he'd always suspected that he'd been set up four years ago, that someone close to him had betrayed him, he hadn't wanted to believe it.

In prison, he'd told himself it didn't matter. That all of that was behind him.

But as he thought about the look Morgan had given him before going back into the house, the image now branded on his mind, he knew it *did* matter—would always matter. He'd been kidding himself if he thought he could forgive and forget—at least not until he found out who had betrayed him.

And Morgan was as good as any place to start.

JACKLYN SHOULD HAVE SAVED her breath. Shade Waters was impossible. She'd tried to talk to him, but he seemed distracted as he looked in on one of the horses. She saw him frown and touch the horse's side, apparently surprised to find that it was damp, as if recently ridden.

"Is something wrong?" she asked, noting that he seemed upset.

He shook his head irritably. "I told you. I don't have time for this. Shouldn't you be out looking for the rustlers instead of driving me crazy?" he snapped, then sighed, looking his age for a moment. "I just got a call a few minutes before you got here. Tom Robinson's condition is worse."

Her heart dropped, and instantly she felt guilty, because she'd been praying he would regain consciousness. She'd been counting on Tom being able to identify at least one of the rustlers.

"I'm sorry to hear that," she said, a little surprised how hard Waters was taking the news, given that he would now probably get the Robinson ranch, just as Dillon had said. Was Tom's worsened condition really what had Waters upset?

The rancher didn't seem to hear her as he began to wipe down the horse. Jacklyn wondered where Pete Barclay was.

She let herself out of the barn, knowing she wasn't going to get anywhere with him. But she couldn't shake the feeling that Dillon Savage might be right. Maybe there was more going on than she'd thought.

As she started toward her pickup, what she saw stopped her dead. The truck was empty. Dillon Savage was gone.

Chapter Eight

Jacklyn couldn't believe her eyes. No. For just an instant there, she'd believed Dillon, believed she'd been wrong about him, believed he really was trying to help her catch the rustlers.

What a fool she was!

"Excuse me," she said as she spotted a man trimming a hedge that ran along one side of the ranch house. "Did you happen to notice the man who was waiting in the pickup?" She pointed to her truck.

He nodded, shoving back his hat to wipe the sweat from his forehead. "He said to tell you he'd meet you in town if he missed you."

She raised a brow. Town was twenty miles away. Trying not to show her panic or her fury, she asked, "And how, exactly, was he planning to get back to town? Did he say?"

The man shrugged. "He said he needed to take a walk."

Take a walk? Oh, he'd taken a walk all right. She would kill him when she found him. And she *would* find him.

She thanked the gardener and, hoping Shade Waters wasn't watching, tried not to storm to the pickup. There were going to be enough people saying I told you so, starting with Waters.

As she climbed in and started the engine, she looked down the long dirt road. Empty. Just like the truck.

Still fighting panic and fury, she drove until she topped a hill and couldn't see the ranch house anymore. Pulling over, she opened the tracking receiver terminal and started to push the on button, afraid of what she would find.

She knew Dillon Savage. Better than she wanted to. He was too smart. Too charming. Too arrogant for words. But there was something about him, something wounded that had softened her heart to him four years ago, when she'd captured him.

How could he do this? Didn't he realize it was going to get him sent back to prison? Unless he thought he could evade her as he had for so long before.

But the only way he could do that was to disable the monitoring device or cut the thing out. If he had, she'd be lucky if she ever saw him again.

She wasn't even thinking about her career or her anger as she turned on the receiver terminal, her heart in her throat. In those few seconds, she felt such a sense of dread and disappointment that she only got more angry—angry at feeling anything at all for this man.

Until that moment, she hadn't realized how badly she wanted to believe in his innocence.

The steady beep from the terminal startled her. "I'll be…" According to this, he was still on the ranch—and moving in her direction.

Or at least his monitoring device was.

If she drove on up the road, she should connect with him about a half mile from here.

Why would he head for the road, when he could have gotten lost in the mountains and led her on a wild-goose chase? One that she wouldn't have been able to hide from her boss?

As she topped the next rise, she spotted a figure walking nonchalantly across open pasture, headed for the road. He had to have heard the pickup approaching, and yet he didn't look up. Nor did he make any attempt to run away.

He vaulted over the barbed wire fence as she brought the truck to a dust-boiling stop next to him.

She was out of the vehicle, her hand on the butt of her pistol, before he reached the road.

"Don't you ever do that again," she shouted at him.

He held up both hands in surrender.

Had he grinned, she feared she would have pulled the pistol and shot him.

"I'm sorry. I couldn't very well tell you where I was going under the circumstances," he said contritely.

"Circumstances?"

"You were with Shade Waters, and I didn't want him to know I was following one of his stock trucks."

She stared at Dillon. "Why would you follow one of the Waters's stock trucks?" she demanded suspiciously.

"To see what was going on." He glanced up as if he heard someone coming. "Could we talk about this somewhere besides the middle of a county road?"

She sighed, torn between anger and overwhelming relief. She removed her hand from her gun butt and turned back toward the pickup. She'd left the driver's door open. As she slid behind the wheel, he climbed in the passenger side and saw the monitoring device on the seat between them.

"Thought I'd skipped out on you, did you?" He chuckled. "So much for trust. You want me to help you catch these guys? Then you have to give me a little leeway. Keep me on too short a leash and I'm useless to you."

She wasn't so sure he wasn't useless to her, anyway. "So why did you follow the stock truck?"

"I went for a little walk. Took your binoculars," he said, handing them back to her. "Hope you don't mind. I just happened to see a couple of ranch hands loading something into the back of a stock truck. They acted suspicious, you know? Looking around a lot. I made sure they didn't see me, and when the truck stopped so one could open the gate, I hopped in the back."

As she got the pickup moving, she looked over at Dillon, convinced he was either lying or crazy or both. Then she caught a whiff of his clothing and wrinkled her nose. "Let me guess what was in the back. Something dead."

"Half-a-dozen dead calves."

She shot him a look, the truck swerving on the gravel road. "They were probably just taking them to the dump."

He shook his head. "They were headed north. Waters's dump is to the south."

"He probably has a new dump since you've been here," she said irritably. "Why would you get in the truck with the dead calves?"

He lifted a brow. "*Six* dead calves. Doesn't that make even *you* suspicious?"

Everything made her suspicious. Especially him. "Every rancher loses a few calves—"

"Six all dead at the same time? Not unless they're sick with something."

She glanced over at him. "What do you think killed them?"

"Lead poisoning." He grinned at her obvious surprise. "That's right, Jack, they each had a bullet hole right between their eyes. But that's not the best part. They were missing a patch of hide—right where their brands should have been—and notches had been cut in their ears. You guessed it, no ear tags."

She slammed on the brakes, bringing the

truck to another jarring stop. "What are you talking about?"

He nodded, still grinning. "I knew Shade Waters was still up to no good."

Jacklyn was shaking her head. "You went looking for trouble, didn't you? This walk you took, you just happened along on a stock truck with six possibly rustled dead calves? Where was this?"

"A mile or so from the ranch house."

Her brows shot up.

"I walk fast. I figured I'd be back before you finished with Waters. I told the gardener so you wouldn't worry. I'm telling you the truth, Jack. I swear."

She glared at him and turned back to her driving, not believing anything he said. "So who were these ranch hands?"

"I didn't get a good look at them. When the truck started moving, I took off running, so I could jump in the back."

"Right. But you're sure they work for Waters?" she asked, trying to rein in her temper.

"They were on his land, driving one of his stock trucks," Dillon said.

She could hear the steel in his voice. She shot him a suspicious look. He had to realize that all she had was his word for this, and right now her trust in him was more than a little shaky.

"And you have no idea where they were taking the calves," she said.

"No," he replied through gritted teeth. "North. I would assume to bury them. Look, under other circumstances, I would have stayed with that truck till the end. But I knew you'd flip if you came out and found me gone." His gaze narrowed. "And you did."

"I could have tracked you and the truck," she pointed out.

"I thought of that. But I also really didn't want every lawman in the county coming after me, ready to shoot to kill, before I got to explain that I hadn't just taken off. Even you believed that's what I'd done, didn't you?"

He was right. Even if she'd had faith that he wouldn't run off, Stratton would have had a warrant out on Dillon Savage before the ink dried.

"Plus I had no weapon and was a little concerned about when the truck got to its destination," Dillon said. "I didn't want to end up buried with those calves. For all I knew they might have been meeting more ranch hands up the road."

If he was telling the truth, he'd done the

only thing he could do. And if so, he'd certainly made more progress than she had in the case.

"I'm sorry," she said. "You did the right thing." She could feel his gaze on her.

"You believe me then?"

She glanced back at him. "Let's say I'm considering the possibility that you're telling the truth."

To her surprise, he laughed. "Jack, you're killing me. But at least that's progress." He turned toward her. "Don't you see, this proves what I've been saying. Waters is your man. He's behind this rustling ring."

She met his gaze, knowing he was capable of making up this whole thing to even the score with his archenemy. "You can't be objective when it comes to Waters."

"There's a reason his ranch hasn't been hit by the rustlers and you know it," Dillon said.

She shook her head. All she knew was that if Dillon was behind the rustling, then by not stealing from Waters, he would make him look guilty. Just as coming up with a story about a stock truck filled with bullet-ridden calves missing their brands would do.

"You're trying to tell me that Waters is

rustling cattle from his neighbors, then killing them, cutting off the brands and ear tags and burying them? Why? He's not even making any money, that I can see, on the deal."

Dillon rolled his eyes. "Waters doesn't need the money. I told you there was another motive. He's getting something out of this, trust me."

She shook her head. "I know you believe he was the cause of your father losing his ranch, but you have to realize there were other factors." She saw his jaw tighten.

"I do. Dad made some business mistakes after my mother died. But ultimately, Waters wanted our ranch and he got it."

"Exactly. He's bought up almost all of the ranches around him, so what—"

"There are still two he wants. And with Tom Robinson gone, he's got that one. That leaves the Harper place."

"Reda will never sell," Jacklyn said, remembering her visit to the Harper ranch when she was talking to local folks about the rustlers. "She hates Waters. Maybe worse than you do."

Dillon lifted a brow. "We'll see. Tom said he'd never sell, either. Jack, we have to get on Waters's ranch and find out where they're taking those calves. You want evidence? It's on the W Bar."

"And what do you suggest I do? Trespass? Waters has already said he won't have us on his ranch."

Dillon grinned. "We need to make Waters think we aren't anywhere near his ranch."

"If you're suggesting—"

"You have to make sure everyone believes you've gotten a new lead and will be to the south, nowhere near the W Bar."

She shook her head. "Stratton would never let me do that."

"That's why you have to tell him you got a tip that the Murray ranch is going to be hit."

"Lie?" Jacklyn fought the sick feeling in the pit of her stomach. "Are you trying to set me up?" she asked, her voice little more than a whisper.

Dillon didn't answer. She looked over at him and saw anger as hard as granite in his blue eyes. "Waters is your man. You want to catch the rustlers?"

She couldn't even acknowledge that with a response.

"When are you going to trust me? I'll tell you what. Let's put something on it. A small wager."

"I don't want your money."

"Don't worry, you won't get it. No, I was thinking of something more fun."

She shot him a warning look.

"A dance. If I'm right, you'll owe me a dance."

"And if you're wrong and it turns out you're involved with this rustling ring?" she asked, studying him as she headed for Lewistown.

He grinned. "Then I'll be back in prison. What do you have to lose? One dance. Deal?"

Was he that sure she'd never prove he was involved? Or was he really innocent—this time? "Deal," she said, ninety-nine percent certain she would never be dancing with Dillon Savage, and a little sad about it.

"So are you going to take my advice?" he said as they shook on their bet.

Not a chance. Waters didn't want her on his ranch. She'd have to get a warrant to go there and she had no evidence to get Stratton to go along with it, not to mention a judge.

"There's a meeting of the ranchers this evening in town," she said noncommittally. "Let's see how that goes."

REDA HARPER CHECKED the time on the dash of her pickup as she cut across her pasture, opened a gate posted with No Trespassing signs and, thumbing her nose at Waters and his W Bar Ranch, drove along what once had been a section road between his spread and the Savage Ranch.

The road had long since grown over with weeds, but Reda was in one of her moods, and when she got like this, she just flat-out refused to drive past the W Bar ranch house. She not only didn't want to see Shade Waters, she also didn't want him seeing her.

As she drove, darkness settled in, forcing her to turn on her headlights. The last thing she wanted was to be caught trespassing on Shade's land. Her own fault. As it would be if she was late for the meeting Shade Waters had called about the rustling problem.

"If you're late, it's your own blamed fault for being so stubborn," she told herself as her pickup jostled along. "You should have taken the main road. Shade is probably already in town, anyway. Damn foolish woman."

On the other hand, it aggravated her that she had to take the back roads to town to avoid seeing Shade Waters. Just the thought of him angered her. She would blame him if she got caught trespassing on his land. But then, she blamed him for most everything that had happened to her in the last forty years.

She blamed herself for being a fool in the first place. What had she ever seen in Shade? Sure, he'd been handsome back then. Hell, downright charming when he'd wanted to be.

She swore at even the thought of him. It still made her sick to think about it. She hated to admit she could have been so stupid. Shade Waters had played her. Tempting her with sweet words and deeds, then reeling her in. His professed love for her nothing more than an attempt to take her ranch.

But in the end, she'd outfoxed him, she reminded herself.

As she came over a rise in the road, she saw a light flicker ahead, off to her left. She frowned as the light flashed off, pitching the terrain back into darkness—but not before her headlights had caught a stock truck pulling behind a rock bluff a good twenty yards inside the fence line.

There was nothing on this road for miles. Nothing but sagebrush and rock. Shade didn't run cattle up here. Never had. Too close to the badlands. Too hard to round 'em all up. Not to mention he had so much land he didn't need to pasture his cattle in the vicinity.

So what would a stock truck be doing up here? As far as she knew, no one used this road. Hadn't since Waters bought the Savage Ranch.

She slowed. In her headlights, she could see where the truck had trampled the grass as it drove back between the bluffs. How odd.

Reda powered down her window, pulling the pickup to a stop to stare out. The night was black. No moon. The stars muted by wisps of clouds. She couldn't see a damn thing. If she hadn't seen the light, she would never have known there was a truck out there among the rocks.

What had her curiosity going was the way the truck had disappeared, as if the driver didn't want to be seen.

The air that wafted in the window was warm and scented with dust and sage. She listened. Not a sound. And yet she'd seen the light. Knew there was a truck in there somewhere.

She felt a cold chill and shuddered as a thought struck her. Whoever was there hadn't expected anyone on this road tonight. The driver had turned out the lights when he'd seen her come flying over the rise. For some reason he hadn't heard her approaching.

Whatever he was doing, he didn't want a witness.

Reda knew, probably better than anyone in four counties, what Waters was capable of. But she had a feeling this wasn't his doing.

On a sudden impulse, she reached for the gearshift and the button to power up her window, telling herself she wanted no part of whatever was going on.

But as the window started to glide upward, she heard a sound behind her pickup, like the scuff of a boot sole on a rock.

Her foot tromped down on the gas pedal. The tires spat dirt and chunks of grass as she took off, her blood pounding in her ears, her hands shaking.

When she glanced into her rearview mirror, she saw the black outline of a man standing in the middle of the road.

He'd been right behind her truck.

She was shaking so hard she had trouble digging her cell phone from her purse while keeping the pickup on the road between the fence posts.

Was it possible he was one of the rustlers?

Her cell phone display read No Service. She swore and tossed the phone back into her purse. Worthless thing. She only used the damn gadget to call from town to the ranch. Only place she could get any reception.

She glanced behind her again, afraid she'd see lights. Or worse, the dark silhouette of a stock truck chasing her without its headlights on.

But the road behind her was empty.

She drove as fast as she dared, telling herself she had to notify someone. Not Shade Waters, even though it was his property. It would be a cold day in hell if she ever spoke to him again.

No, she'd drive straight to the meeting. Sheriff McCray would be there. She'd tell him what she'd seen.

Her pulse began to slow as she checked her mirror again and saw no one following her. Even in the dark, she would have been able to see the huge shape of a stock truck on the road. She was pretty darn sure she could outrun a cattle truck.

As she swung into the packed lot at the community center, she felt a little calmer. More rational.

Maybe it had been rustlers. Maybe not. Shade Waters was the only rancher who hadn't lost cattle to that band of thieves she'd been hearing about. It made sense that the rustlers had finally gotten around to stealing some of his livestock.

Except that Waters wasn't running any cattle in that area.

Reda parked and headed for the meeting. As she pushed open the door to the community center, the first man she saw was Sheriff Claude McCray. She started to rush to him, her mouth already open as she prepared to tell him about what she'd seen on the road.

But then she saw the man he was deep in conversation with: Shade Waters. Their heads were together as if they were cooking up something.

Her mouth snapped shut, the words gone like dead leaves blowing away in the wind. She walked past both men, her head held high. The sheriff didn't seem to notice her, but Shade Waters did.

She could feel his gaze on her, as intense and burning as a laser beam. She waltzed right on past without even a twinge of guilt. She hoped the rustlers cleaned Shade Waters out. Hell, she wished she had stopped and helped them.

ON THE DRIVE BACK to Lewistown, Jack had seemed lost in thought, which was just fine with Dillon. He tried not to think about Waters or the fact that Jack didn't believe him. Those problems aside, he couldn't get Morgan Landers off his mind—or the fact that she was apparently now with Nate Waters.

Jack stopped by the hospital to see how Tom Robinson was doing, and Dillon went in with her even though he hated to. The last time he'd been in a hospital was after his father's heart attack.

The moment he walked in, he was hit by the smell. It took him back instantly, filling him with grief and guilt. His father would have been only fifty-eight now, young by today's standards, if he had lived. If Shade Waters hadn't killed him as surely as if he'd held a gun to his head.

Tom was still unconscious. His recovery didn't look good, which meant that the chances of him identifying the rustlers wasn't good, either.

Dillon could see the effect that had on Jack. She'd been counting on a break in the rustling case. As they left the hospital, he could feel her anger and frustration.

"Would you please stop looking at me as if I was the one who put Tom in that hospital bed?" Dillon said as she drove back toward the motel.

"Aren't you?"

He groaned. "Jack, I'm telling you I have nothing to do with this bunch of rustlers. You've got to believe that." But of course, she didn't have to.

She shot him a quizzical look. Clearly, she didn't believe anything he said.

"How can I convince you?" he asked. "We already know who the rustler is, but you don't believe that, either. I told you what we have to do to catch him, except you aren't willing to do that. So what else can I say?" He shook his head.

"Don't you find it interesting that some of your old friends are working ranches around here?" she asked.

So she'd been thinking about some of the cowboys he'd run around with: Pete Barclay, Buford Cole, Arlen Dubois.

"*Former* friends," he said. "We haven't been close for years. A lifetime ago."

"I know for a fact that Buford Cole came to visit you in prison."

It shouldn't have taken him by surprise, but it did. Of course she would have checked to see who his visitors had been during his four years at Montana State Prison.

"Buford and I used to be close," he admitted. "He only came that one time. I haven't heard from him since."

"What about Pete Barclay?"

Dillon chuckled. "Yeah, he came to visit me in prison several times."

"He works for Waters."

"I'm aware of that. You want to know why he came to see me?" Dillon asked. "To deliver threats from his boss about when I got out."

She swung her gaze to him. "Is that true?"

"I told you I don't lie."

"Right. How could I forget?" She pulled into the motel parking lot and glanced at her watch. "We have to get to the ranchers' meeting. I just need to change." She settled her gaze on him. "Maybe you shouldn't go. You could stay in the motel room. You'd be monitored the whole time, of course."

"Of course," he said disagreeably. He hated to be reminded of how little freedom he had. Or how little trust she had in him. Not that he could blame her. He hated being constantly watched. But that was the deal, wasn't it?

"I'm going with you," he said, meeting her gaze head-on.

"I'm not sure that's a good idea."

"I'm not afraid of any of them, and I have nothing to hide."

She gave him one of her rock-hard looks, as if nothing could move her.

"Jack, come on. You think I have that much control over everything that is happening now?" He couldn't help but smile and shake his head. "You give me too much credit."

"On the contrary. I think you are capable of just about anything you set your mind to."

He made a face, recognizing his own words to her earlier. "That almost sounded like a compliment," he joked. "So you got me out of prison thinking you'd give me enough rope that I'd hang myself? That's it, isn't it?" He saw that he'd hit too close to home, and chuckled at her expression.

"If not you, then who?" she demanded. "And don't tell me Shade Waters." She cocked an eyebrow at him, her eyes the color of gunmetal. There was a pleading in her expression. "Whoever is leading this band of rustlers is too good at this. Is it possible there is someone who's even better than the great Dillon Savage?"

He shrugged, but admitted to himself that she had a point. Waters was a lot of things, but what did he know about rustling? Whoever was leading the ring knew what he was doing. But if it wasn't Shade Waters, was it someone who worked for him?

Chapter Nine

The lot was full of pickups as Jacklyn tried to find a place to park at the community center. Clearly, many ranchers had arrived early, not about to miss this.

She couldn't help but think it was the last place Dillon wanted to be. She looked around for a large tree, figuring one of the ranchers might have a rope and this could end in a hangin' before the night was over. And it would be Dillon Savage's neck in the noose.

"I'd prefer if you don't say anything during the meeting," she said as she cut the engine and looked over at him.

"No problem." He glanced toward the building. All the lights were on and a muted roar came from inside. A few ranchers were out on the steps, smoking and talking in the darkness. They'd all glanced toward the state pickup as she'd parked.

"You sure about this?" she asked.

"If I don't go in," Dillon said, "they'll assume you're trying to protect me."

That was exactly what she hoped to do. "Maybe I'm trying to protect us both."

He smiled at that. "We're both more than capable of taking care of ourselves."

She wasn't so sure. The ranchers were furious. Shade Waters had them all stirred up about Dillon being out of prison. And unfortunately, Dillon had enemies in there waiting for him—and so did she.

Jacklyn stepped from the pickup, her hand going to the gun at her hip as she started toward the community center and the angry-looking men now blocking the doorway. Dillon walked next to her. She dreaded the moment he would come face-to-face with Shade Waters, not sure what either of them would do.

The men on the steps finally parted so she and Dillon could enter. The room was already buzzing as she pushed open the door. She wasn't surprised to find the center packed, a sea of Stetsons.

As she started down the aisle between the chairs, she could feel Dillon right behind her. A wave of stunned silence seemed to fill the place, followed at once by a louder buzzing of voices as heads turned. They hadn't expected her to bring Dillon. He'd been right about coming.

She didn't look at any of them as she made her way toward the front of the room. But Shade Waters stopped her before she could reach it. "No one invited you. Or your *friend.*"

Dillon Savage was far from her friend, but she wasn't here to debate that with Waters.

"I'm here to clear up a few things," she said over the drone of voices.

"Things are damn clear," Waters said angrily. "The state isn't doing a thing to protect us ranchers."

"What's this *us?*" called a female voice from near the front. "Your cattle haven't been stolen. So what are you all worked up about?"

Jacklyn recognized the strident voice as Reda Harper's.

"You think my ranch isn't next?" Waters demanded to the crowd, apparently ignoring Reda. "Only it won't be fifty head of cattle. The bastards will hit me harder than any of you, and we all know it."

"That's why I'm here," Jacklyn said. "So that doesn't happen. But just this afternoon you denied me access to your land."

There were murmurs from the crowd.

"And you know damn well why," Waters snapped, glaring at Dillon.

Was Dillon the reason? Or was he telling the truth and there was a lot more going on here than missing cattle.

"You didn't protect *my* ranch," said an angry male voice.

"You're finally going to do something because it's the W Bar?" called another. "What about the rest of us?"

"Let her talk," cried one of the ranchers.

"Yeah, I'd like to hear what she has to say," Reda declared.

Waters scowled at Jacklyn, visibly upset that she'd come, and maybe even more upset that Reda Harper had been heckling him. He turned his scowl on Dillon and cursed. "I'd like to hear what Dillon Savage has to say for himself," Waters bellowed.

A few in the crowd were agreeing with him as Jacklyn stepped up on the stage. She glanced around the room, recognizing most of the faces. Waters's son, Nate, was slumped in the first row, looking bored.

As she stepped behind the podium, Dillon joined her, standing back but facing the angry crowd.

"Yeah, what the hell is the story?" called out one of the ranchers. "You get a rustler out to catch rustlers? What kind of sense is that?"

She raised a hand. When the room finally quieted, she waited for Shade Waters to sit down, glancing at him pointedly until he took his seat.

"Most of you know me. I'm Stock Detective Jacklyn Wilde," she began. "And I know most of you. Because of that you know I'm doing everything I can to catch the rustlers." She hurried on as the room threatened to erupt again.

"Dillon Savage is helping with the investigation of the rustling ring operating in this area." As expected, a wave of protests rang out. Again she raised a hand and waited patiently for the room to go quiet.

"I will not debate my decision to have Mr. Savage released early to help in that investigation. You want the rustlers caught?" she demanded, above the shouts and angry accusations. "Then listen to me."

"We've listened to you long enough," Shade Waters said, getting to his feet again. "It's time we took matters into our own hands."

"That's right!" A dozen ranchers were on their feet.

She saw her boss and several others come in through the back door. Chief Brand Inspector Allan Stratton walked up the aisle to the stage and stepped to the podium, practically shoving her aside.

Jacklyn edged back, hating the son of a bitch for upstaging her in front of the ranchers.

"Finally we're going to get some answers," Waters called. "You sent us a damn woman, when we need a man for *this* job."

Others began to applaud Stratton, echoing Waters's sentiments.

Jacklyn felt her face flame. It was all she could do not to walk off the stage. She felt Dillon move to her side, as if in a show of support for her. The move would only antagonize the ranchers, and worse, Sheriff McCray, whom she spotted standing on the sidelines, glaring at her.

Stratton raised his arms and waited for the room to quiet down before he spoke. "I don't have to tell any of you how hard it is to stop rustlers. Livestock are a very lucrative source of income."

There were nods across the room, some murmurs.

"A thief who breaks into a house and steals a television or CD player can try to sell the equipment either at a pawnshop or on the black market, but will likely only get about ten percent of the actual value of the property," Stratton continued. "Someone who steals a cow, on the other hand, can sell the animal at a packing plant or an auction market and receive one hundred percent of the value."

There were more murmurs of agreement, but some restless movement as the smarter ranchers began to realize Stratton wasn't telling them anything they didn't already know.

"Improvements in transportation, the interstate, bigger cattle trailers, all make it easier for criminals to load up cattle and haul them across state lines before you even realize the animals are missing," he continued. "I don't have to tell you that thieves can steal more and move farther and faster than in the old days. A rustler can steal cattle here today, and this afternoon or early tomorrow morning be in Tennessee or California."

"Don't you think we know all that?" one of the ranchers demanded.

"What I can tell you is that we need to

work together to stop these rustlers," Stratton said.

"You know a lot of us can't afford to hire more hands or buy special equipment," a man said from the front row.

"The state can't afford to hire staff to watch your cattle, either," Stratton said, as if it hurt him personally to say that. "That's why we need each of you to help us. Experienced cattle thieves will watch a ranch for a while, get to know the schedule of the owner and hired hands, and the times of day when no one will be around. You can keep an eye out for strangers hanging around or hired help that's too curious."

Jacklyn couldn't believe Stratton thought the rustling gang was that stupid. They weren't like some bumbling amateurs who left a gas receipt or wallet at the scene of the crime. These guys always got away clean. Except possibly for a good-luck coin. And even that could have been dropped by anyone at any time.

But for sure, the rustlers wouldn't be asking stupid questions of ranchers.

"You can also run checks on the men you hire," Stratton was saying, over an uproar from the floor. "I know society is so mobile that you're lucky to get a ranch hand to stay a season, let alone longer, and most ranches don't keep good records when it comes to seasonal help."

The crowd was getting restless.

Stratton had to raise his voice as he explained how every rancher should brand even dairy cows. "One white or black cow looks exactly like another. We have no way of telling them apart."

"I thought some states were using DNA?" a rancher asked over the growing murmuring.

"It's expensive, and we have to have some idea where the cow was stolen so we can try to match the DNA," he replied. "The best place to stop rustlers is at livestock sales. We need those people to be attentive. There are also radio-frequency chips that we're looking into. It's an expense for all of you, I know, but—"

"It sounds like you're expecting everyone else to do your job," a rancher called.

"Yeah," Waters agreed. "What's the bottom line here? You're telling us you aren't going to do a damn thing?"

"The only way we can beat the rustlers is to work together." Stratton was forced to yell to be heard over the uproar. "You have to trust—"

Jacklyn walked over to the podium and kicked it over. Stratton jumped back as if he'd been shot. The boom as the podium hit the floor sent a shock wave through the room, instantly quieting everyone. All attention was fixed on her.

She barely had to raise her voice. "You want to know how easy is it to steal your cattle? Simple as hell. If there is nobody watching them tonight, the rustlers are out there taking a dozen, two dozen, three dozen right now. You probably won't even know for weeks, maybe months, that they're gone. As for the rustlers, they made a quick getaway. Your cattle *could* be in another state. Or already butchered. Doesn't matter, because they aren't going to turn up. You just lost ten, twenty thousand dollars."

She looked out at the stunned audience of ranchers. "*That's* the reality. I plan to catch these rustlers. But even if I do, there will be others. Unless you help, we'll never be able to protect your property. That, Mr. Waters, is the bottom line."

With that she turned and walked off the stage as the room went from stunned silence to a clamor of voices. She saw a group of ranchers corner Stratton, blocking his exit, as she and Dillon slipped out the side into the cool darkness.

DILLON LET OUT a low whistle as he joined her outside. "You all right?"

She'd stopped at the street, as if she'd forgotten where she'd parked the truck. When he touched her shoulder, he could feel her shaking.

"I'm fine." She took a step forward to break the contact, but made no move toward the pickup.

"That was great back there. You got the respect of every man in that room."

A small sound like a chuckle came out of her. "*That* just cost me my job."

"No way. The bastard tried to make you look bad, and only succeeded in ticking off everyone in the center. He won't come at you like that again. And once you catch the rustlers…"

She spun on him, her face contorting in anger. "You know damn well I'm not going to catch the rustlers. It's the only reason you agreed to pretend to help me."

"You're wrong."

"Damn it, Dillon, I know you're the one who's leading them. It's how they keep one step ahead of me. Just like you used to."

He shook his head. "You're wrong about that, too."

The anger was gone as quickly as it had appeared. "It doesn't matter now, anyway."

"The hell you say. Come on, Jack. We can do this. I'll help you. Really help you. After all, it's the only way I can prove to you how wrong you are about me."

She seemed to study him in the lamplight. Behind him, the community center was in an uproar. "How can I trust you?"

He smiled. "You can buy me a steak. Come on," he said again, as some of the ranchers began to leave the meeting. "There's a steak house just a short walk from here. I don't know about you, but I could use some fresh air." He took her arm before she could object, and they started down the street. It was a good walk, but he figured they both could use it.

Also, he didn't want a run-in with the ranchers. Not for himself, but for Jacklyn. She'd been through enough tonight. He saw her look over at him as if trying to make up her mind about him.

Funny, but at that moment he wanted to be

the man his father always told him he could
be. The last thing Dillon wanted to do was
disappoint Jacklyn Wilde.

Unfortunately, there was little chance of
him doing anything *but* disappointing her.

JACKLYN COULDN'T BELIEVE she'd let Dillon
talk her into this.

"After everything you've been through
tonight, I say we celebrate," he'd said as they
walked into the steak house.

"Celebrate?" Had he lost his mind?

"You still have a job. I'm not on my way
to prison. Yet," he added with a grin. "Tell me
that isn't cause for celebration."

She might have argued that keeping her
job was nothing to celebrate. Maybe Dillon
was right. Maybe she was a fool for thinking
that her job mattered. Right now not even the
ranchers thought so.

The steak house was crowded, especially at
the bar. They were shown to a booth in the
rear. She noticed that Dillon made a point of
sitting with his back to the wall rather than the
room. Something he'd picked up in prison?

To her surprise, the waitress put a bottle of
her favorite wine on the table and a cold beer
in front of Dillon, no glass.

She looked up at him in surprise.

He grinned. "I grabbed a waitress on the way in and told her it was urgent."

"How did you—"

"Know your favorite wine?" His grin broadened. "It's not my psychic ability. I asked. It's what you ordered the last time you were in here. Apparently, you made an impression."

She groaned inwardly. The last time was right before she'd gotten Dillon out of prison. She'd been feeling anything but confident about her decision, and had definitely imbibed more than she should have. No wonder the waitress remembered what wine she'd ordered.

Dillon poured her a glass of wine, then lifted his bottle of beer in a toast, his gaze locked with hers. "To a successful collaboration."

She slowly picked up the glass, clinked it softly against his beer bottle and took a sip, not any more sure of the appropriateness of the toast than she was about drinking even one glass of wine with Dillon Savage.

He took a long swallow of his beer, then stared at the bottle, his thumb making patterns on the sweating glass. "I can't remember the last beer I had." He looked up, scanning the noisy steak house and bar. "It still all feels surreal."

Just then a man who'd had too much to drink stumbled into their table, startling them both and jostling her glass and spilling some of the wine. But it was Dillon's instant reaction that startled her the most.

In a flash, he'd grabbed the beer bottle by its neck, brandishing it like a weapon as he shot to his feet, ready to defend himself and her.

The drunken man raised both hands. "Sorry. My apologies," he said, backing away. "Just clumsy. No harm done, right?"

Dillon sat back down, turning the bottle as he did and gently setting it on the table as beer spilled down the sides. He'd gone pale, his eyes wide. She thought she saw his hand shaking as he rubbed it over his face. "Old habits die hard," he said quietly. "Sorry."

She stared at him, shocked by how quickly he'd changed when he'd felt threatened. "Was it that dangerous in there?" she asked, before she could stop herself.

He looked up at her, his grimace slow and almost painful. "Prison? Dangerous? With people who are crazy, mean, strung out?" He shook his head. "What makes it dangerous is a lack of hope. A lot of those people will never see the outside again and they know it. Because of that, they have nothing to lose."

He smiled as if to lighten his words. "If you're smart, you do your time, stay out of trouble, make the right friends." He grinned. "Like I said, I make friends easily, and you know what they say. What doesn't kill you makes you stronger."

She heard something in his tone that tore at her heart.

The waitress hurried over to mop up the mess, then returned with another beer for Dillon. "That gentleman over there sends his apologies," she said.

Dillon looked in the drunken man's direction and gave a nod.

Jacklyn took a drink of her wine to try to wash down the lump in her throat, and busied herself with her menu. What was wrong with her, having sympathy for a criminal? A criminal *she'd* put behind bars? Dillon had the same options as everyone else. He didn't have to rustle cattle. He'd chosen the route that had led him straight to prison. He had only himself to blame.

So how could she feel sorry for him?

Because, she thought, lowering her menu to peer across the table at him, Dillon Savage wasn't the criminal stereotype. Instead he was educated, smart, from a good family. And, she suspected, a man with his own code of ethics. So what had made him turn to crime?

She tried to concentrate on her menu, but when she looked up again, she saw that Dillon was no longer gazing at his. Instead, he was staring toward the bar, a strange expression on his face.

She turned to follow his gaze. A few cowboys were standing together, the back door closing as someone left. All she caught sight of was one denim-clad shoulder and a glimpse of a western hat.

She searched the group at the bar and recognized only Arlen Dubois, from earlier today on Tom Robinson's ranch.

Was that who Dillon had noticed? Or had it been whoever had just left? In any case, Dillon looked upset.

"Who was that?" she asked, turning back to him.

His expression instantly changed, to an innocent look. "I beg your pardon?"

"You saw someone, someone you recognized?" He'd spotted someone he hadn't wanted to see. She was sure of it. She tried to read his expression, but his eyes showed only the vast blue of an endless sky. She would have thought she was wrong about him seeing someone he knew if it hadn't been for the twitch of a muscle along his jaw.

He was looking at her now, studying her the way she'd been studying him. He always seemed slightly amused—and wary.

THE WOMAN WAS PERCEPTIVE. Much more than Dillon had realized. He smiled at her, meeting her gaze, cranking up the charm as he tried to mask whatever had alerted her.

"What makes you think I wasn't just staring off into space, thinking about the meeting tonight and Shade Waters?"

She cocked her head, her look one of disappointment. "How about the truth? Try it, you might like it."

He rubbed the back of his neck and smiled faintly at her.

"The person who just left. You knew him."

He frowned. "What would make you think that?"

"Don't play games with me," she snapped. "And stop answering my questions with one of your own."

"Okay," he said. "What say we flip for it?" He pulled a quarter from his pocket and spun it between his fingers. "A little wager of sorts. Truth for truth."

"You like to gamble, don't you?"

He grinned. "I like to take my chances sometimes, yes. And I never lie, remember?"

She drew a breath, her gaze on the silver flicker of the quarter in the dim light of the restaurant. "Is it that hard for you to tell the truth that you have to flip for it?"

He did his best to look offended. "Don't assume just because I have a proclivity for cattle rustling that I'm a liar—and a gambler."

"Of course not."

He turned serious for a moment. "Have I ever lied to you?"

She met his gaze. "How would I know?"

"You could look into my eyes." His gaze locked with hers. "So what do you say? A flip of the coin. Heads, I tell you whatever you want to know. Tails, you tell me something I'd like to know."

She watched the quarter for a moment, then held out her hand. "I'll flip the coin if you don't mind."

He pretended to be hurt by her lack of trust. "You'll answer truthfully?"

He nodded. "And you?"

"I'm always honest."

He smiled at that. "I guess we'll see about that."

Jacklyn didn't like the gleam in his eyes, but anything was better than talking about his prison stay. She'd seen a side of him with the drunken man that had scared her, and at the same time made her want to comfort him.

Fear of Dillon Savage was good—and appropriate. Sympathy on any level was dangerous.

Probably as dangerous as this game he had her playing. But against her better judgment, she believed him when he said he'd tell her the truth if she won the coin toss. And since she was no doubt going to get fired before the night was over, and Dillon would be going back to prison, what did it hurt?

He was watching her, humor dancing in his eyes, as she inspected the coin. "You're the least trusting woman I've ever known."

"Then the women you've known didn't know you very well."

He laughed. It was a nice sound. He took a long drink of his beer and seemed to relax. She hadn't noticed, but apparently he'd refilled her wineglass.

It crossed her mind that he might be trying to get her drunk. She met his gaze, then tossed the coin up, catching it and bringing it down flat on the tabletop.

He took on an excited, eager look as he stared down at her hand and waited for her to lift it from the coin.

Drawing a breath, she did so, instantly relieved to see it was heads.

She smiled at him and took a drink of her wine.

He leaned back, raising his hands in defeat and grinning. "You win, and I'm a man of honor whether you believe it or not. So what do you want to know? The truth, I swear."

"Who did you see earlier going out the back door?"

He glanced toward the bar, clearly hesitating, then slowly said, "Truthfully? I'm not even sure. I just caught a glimpse of the man. Actually, it was the way he moved. It reminded me of someone I used to know. But it couldn't have been him, because he's dead."

She eyed Dillon suspiciously. "What was his name?"

"Halsey Waters." Dillon met her gaze, and she saw pain and anger. "I guess it's because I've been thinking about him."

"He was a good friend?"

Dillon nodded. "We were best friends. He was like a brother to me. I've never been that close to anyone since." He smiled ruefully. "Just one of those regrets in life, you know what I mean?"

"Yes," she said, and looked toward the bar, wondering who Dillon had seen that might remind him of Halsey Waters. Or if he'd made up the whole thing.

"Trust," he said, with his usual amusement.

Then Morgan Landers walked in the door with Nate Waters.

Chapter Ten

Jacklyn couldn't very well miss the instant that Dillon saw Morgan. His entire demeanor changed. Like him, she watched the two come in on a cool gust of night air, Morgan laughing, Nate totally absorbed in her.

When Jacklyn turned back to Dillon, he was on his feet, excusing himself to go to the restroom. He walked away, not looking back. Jacklyn turned, pretty sure she'd find Morgan watching Dillon go, but her view was blocked by a man standing next to her table.

"Jacklyn Wilde?" he asked, but before she could answer he slid into the seat Dillon had just vacated. "I'm Buford Cole. A friend of Dillon's."

She studied the man across from her. He looked like most of the other cowboys, wearing jeans, boots, a western shirt and hat. His face was weathered from a life outdoors, and crow's-feet bracketed his brown eyes.

"How much do you know about Dillon Savage?" Buford asked before she could comment.

His question took her by surprise. "Not much," she said, telling herself how true that was.

"He ever tell you how he got into rustling cattle?" Buford didn't wait for an answer. "Dillon believes that his family's ranch was stolen."

"Stolen?" she asked, even though she knew that's how Dillon felt.

Buford nodded. "Cattle disappeared, others got accidentally closed off from water and died. There were a lot of strange accidents around the ranch, including his father's near-death accident that left him dependent on a cane. After that his dad just gave up. His spread was bought by Shade Waters. Dillon's always believed his father died of a broken heart. That ranch was his life."

She'd suspected as much.

"But even if Dillon believed that Shade Waters stole his family ranch, why not alert the authorities or just steal cattle from the

W Bar if he wanted revenge?" she asked. "Why steal from all his neighbors?"

"Dillon's father tried to get the neighboring ranchers to join forces and fight Waters. They all turned a blind eye to what was happening on the Savage Ranch. By the time it started happening to them, Dillon's old man was dead, the ranch lost. Then Waters bought up one ranch after another, usually after each had had its share of bad luck."

"Are you trying to tell me that Waters—"

"I'm trying to tell you what Dillon believes," Buford interrupted, glancing toward the hallway to the restrooms where Dillon had disappeared. "In the end, all but two of the ranchers sold out to Waters."

"Why, if what Dillon believes is true, weren't those two forced to sell as well then?"

"You ever meet Reda Harper? As for Tom Robinson, he was barely hanging on by a thread. Now after what happened…" The cowboy shook his head. "Word is that Waters has already bought it from Tom Robinson's niece. As for Reda… She's old. Waters can wait her out."

"You sound as if you don't like Shade Waters any more than Dillon does."

"I don't like fighting battles I know I can't

win. Dillon's an idealist. He still believes in justice. And vengeance."

"You think Dillon is out for revenge?" she asked, thinking about the ranchers that Dillon had rustled cattle from. They'd all later sold out to Waters. When she'd finally caught him, he'd been on the W Bar, Shade's own ranch. She'd thought Dillon had gotten greedy and that had been his downfall. Now she wondered.

She'd seen how much Waters and Dillon hated each other, but the big rancher's hatred of Dillon seemed out of proportion to the amount of cattle he'd lost over the years.

"Why does Shade hate Dillon so much?" she asked, feeling the effects of the wine.

"Did you ask Dillon?"

She shook her head.

"Shade Waters blames him for his son's death."

"Halsey," she murmured, frowning to herself. "But he was Dillon's best friend."

Buford smiled at that. "We were all friends. Did you ever wonder what happened to the cattle Dillon rustled?" he asked. "Dillon put them in with Waters's herd."

She stared at him. Wouldn't she have heard this from Waters if that were true?

The cowboy chuckled. "The cattle just

seemed to disappear. Who knows what Waters did with them."

Jacklyn thought about the dead calves in the stock truck that Dillon swore had been shot. Is that what Shade Waters had done with the rustled cattle he'd found among his herd?

And then what? Just taken them out and buried them?

What a waste. And for what?

She couldn't believe the lengths Dillon had gone to. But was any of this true? Or was it just the way he rationalized his thieving ways to his friends?

"You seem to know a lot about Dillon's rustling activities," she said.

Buford smiled. "You aren't going to ask me if I was in on it with him, are you?"

"You were one of his closest friends, right? This gang of rustlers—you think he has anything to do with them?"

Buford looked wary. "I wouldn't know."

"But you think it's possible."

He sighed, still not looking at her. "I just know Dillon isn't finished with Waters." He shook his head as he rose from the booth. "He won't be, either, until Waters is either behind bars or dead. Unfortunately, Dillon Savage is the kind of man who takes a grudge to the grave. I would just hate to see him in an early grave."

Why was Buford telling her all this? Buford appeared to be genuinely worried about his old friend. But didn't he realize this only made Dillon look guilty of being the leader of this latest band of cattle rustlers?

As Buford walked away, Jacklyn saw that Nate Waters was sitting alone. Where was Morgan? And why hadn't Dillon returned?

MORGAN GASPED as Dillon stepped directly into her path. Her hand went to her throat, her eyes looking around wildly as if searching for a way to escape the dim restaurant hallway.

"Dillon."

He smiled as he moved so close he could see the fear in her eyes. "Morgan."

She licked her lips and smiled back nervously. "What are you doing here?" Without Nate Waters beside her, she'd lost a lot of her haughtiness.

"I wanted to see you, Morgan. Don't tell me you didn't expect to meet up with me again."

"I didn't think you could…that is, I thought you weren't allowed to go anywhere alone."

He smiled at that. "Is that what you thought?"

She swallowed, looking again for a way to escape, but he was blocking the hallway. She'd have to go over him to get back to Nate.

"We should get together sometime," she said, shifting nervously. "To talk. A lot has happened since you've been gone."

"So I gather. You and Waters." Dillon shook his head. She would turn Nate any way but loose before she was through.

"Nate and I are getting married."

"You're perfect for each other."

She frowned, thinking he was being facetious.

"Seriously, I wish you all the best."

"You're not upset?" She was eyeing him now, obviously not wanting to believe that he'd gotten over her.

"I had a lot of time to think in prison," he said, his gaze locking with hers. "It cleared up a lot for me. Like, for instance, how I just happened to get caught."

She shifted again, pulling her shoulder bag around to the front, her hand going to it.

He put his hand over hers and smiled. "Carrying a gun now? You have something to fear, Morgan?"

184   *Big Sky Standoff*

Her gaze hardened as she jerked her hand away from his.

"You set me up that day, didn't you?"

She was shaking her head. "You're wrong. I swear to you."

"Come on, Morgan, you were the only person who knew where I would be."

"No, the others knew. It had to be one of them. Or maybe your luck just ran out."

"Yeah, maybe that was it." He reached into her purse and pulled out the gun, swinging the barrel around until the end was pointed at her forehead. Her eyes widened as she heard him snap off the safety.

"Here's the one-time deal," he told her. "The truth for your life. Because, Morgan, I'm going to find out who set me up. Tell me the truth now and I walk away. No foul, no harm. For old time's sake, I'll give you this chance. But," he added quickly, "if I find out you lied, I'll come back and all bets are off. So what's it going to be?"

"I'm telling you the truth. I didn't say a word to anyone. I swear. It wasn't me, Dillon. I couldn't do that to you."

He would have argued the latter, but his time was up. Jacklyn would have realized

by now that he was missing. He couldn't
chance her finding him holding a gun on
Morgan.

He emptied the gun, snapped the safety back
on and dropped the weapon into her purse,
pocketing the bullets. "Wouldn't want you to
accidentally shoot anyone," he said with a grin.

It would have been like Morgan to shoot
him in the back and say it was self-defense.
And with the Waters family behind her, she
would have probably gotten away with it.

"I'm sure we'll be seeing each other again,"
he said.

"Not if I see you first," Morgan snapped
back.

He chuckled to himself as he turned and
walked away. Behind him, Morgan let out a
string of curse words. That's what he'd loved
about her: she was no lady.

Back at the table, Jack seemed relieved to
see him. As Morgan returned to her own
table, Jack shot Dillon a suspicious look.

He picked up his menu and studied it. But
he could feel both Jack and Morgan looking
in his direction. He'd known what kind of
woman Morgan was. The kind who would
lie through her teeth. The fact that she was

carrying a gun didn't bode well in the truth department. She was afraid of someone. Him, no doubt. Which led him to believe she had something to hide.

She'd said the others knew where he'd be that day.

Yes, the others. His friends, his partners, the men he'd trusted with his life. He'd have to have a little talk with each of them. If he helped Jack bust up this rustling ring, he'd get the opportunity, he was sure.

"Have you made up your mind?" Jack asked.

He couldn't help but wonder if Morgan might not be involved. She was carrying a gun and had hooked up with the son of one of the richest and most influential ranchers in the state of Montana.

He looked up from his menu. "Definitely," he said, smiling at her.

"About what you're going to order," she said, but not with her usual irritation at his foolishness.

The wine had mellowed her some. Her cheeks were a little flushed. She looked damn good in candlelight. Dillon had the wildest urge to reach across the table and free her hair from that braid.

The waitress appeared at that moment, saving him. After they'd ordered, he stole a glance in the direction of Morgan's table.

Morgan and Nate were gone.

JACKLYN COULDN'T HELP thinking about everything Buford Cole had told her as she ate her dinner. The wine had left her feeling too warm, too relaxed, too intent on the man across the table from h

Dillon was his usual charming self. And she found herself enjoying not only the meal, but also the company.

But what difference did it make? She was sure she'd lost her job tonight. In fact, she was surprised that Stratton hadn't already called to fire her.

After dinner they walked back toward the community center, both falling into silence as if a spell had been broken. The night was dark and cold. Lewistown was close to the mountains, so that often made nights here chilly, especially in spring.

Without a word, Dillon took off his jacket and put it around her shoulders. She thought about protesting, but was still in that what-the-heck mood.

Tonight he'd sweet-talked her, stood up for

her, wined and dined her, and she'd liked it. In the morning, she'd be her old self again. Not that it mattered. She was sure Stratton would be picking up Dillon to take him back to prison, and would fire her.

What would *she* do? She didn't have a clue. But for some reason not even that bothered her right now.

"Pretty night," Dillon said, as he stopped to look up at the star.

She stopped, too, taking a deep breath of the clean air, feeling strangely happy and content. A dangerous way to be feeling this close to Dillon Savage.

His hand brushed her sleeve, and she turned toward him like a flower to the sun. They were so close she couldn't be sure who made the first move. All she knew was that when his lips brushed hers, she felt sparks.

She leaned into him, wanting more even as the sensible Jackyln Wilde tried to warn her that she'd regret it in the morning. Heck, she'd probably regret it before the night was over.

Dillon pulled back. "Jack, you sure you know what you're doing?"

"This isn't the first time I've kissed someone," she said.

He laughed. "No, I didn't think it was. It's just that—" He looked past her and let out a curse.

She turned and saw her pickup sitting alone in the community center parking lot. Sitting at an odd angle.

"Someone slashed your tires," Dillon said, sounding miserable.

To her surprise, she found she was fighting tears. The slashed tires were the last straw. She marched toward her pickup, angry at the world.

"I'm sure you had nothing to do with this, either," she snapped over her shoulder.

He caught up to her as she reached the truck. She started to open the driver's door to get out her insurance card and call for towing, but he slammed it shut, flattening her back to the side of the vehicle.

"How can you say that?" he demanded, his voice hoarse with emotion. "I was with you all night."

"Right, you have the perfect alibi. You were getting me drunk."

He raised a brow. "Is that what that kiss was about? You just had too much to drink?"

She didn't answer, couldn't. She wanted to push him away, to distance herself from him.

Every instinct told her that Dillon Savage was nothing but trouble. And these feelings she had for him, had had for him years ago when she'd spent days learning everything she could about him, chasing him across Montana and finally coming face-to-face with him, well, they were feelings she was damn determined not to have. Especially now.

"Jack?"

She pushed on his chest with both hands, but he was bigger and stronger than she was, and he had her pinned against the truck with his body.

"Trust me, Jack," he said, his eyes dark with emotion. "I know you want to. Let me prove to you that I'm through with that life."

Her eyes filled with tears. She wanted to believe him. But she'd seen the other look in his eyes, the hatred, the need for vengeance. He would never forget that she'd put him in prison. No matter if she believed anything Buford had told her, she believed Dillon Savage was a man who held a grudge.

"Damn it, Jack," he said with a groan. He dragged her to him, his mouth on hers, his arms surrounding her and pulling her in.

He caught her off guard. Just like the first time he'd kissed her, the day she'd captured him. Her lips parted now of their own accord. Just as they had the first time. And just like the first time, she felt the stars and planets fall into line.

Noise erupted from a bar down the street. Dillon stepped back as abruptly as he'd kissed her. She followed his gaze, surprised and disappointed that he'd ended the kiss.

That is, until she saw the lone man standing outside the bar, watching them. As he scratched a match across his boot and lifted the flame to the cigarette dangling from his mouth, his face was caught in the light.

Sheriff Claude McCray.

DILLON FELT SHAKEN. He'd seen the look on the sheriff's face. All Dillon had done was bring Jack more trouble—as if she needed it.

Worse, she'd given him nothing but silence and distance ever since. But at that moment he would have done anything to convince Jack she was wrong about him. As if a kiss would do that! And yet, it had been one hell of a kiss. He'd felt a connection between them. Just as he had the first time. It had haunted him for the past four years, locked up in prison.

Just as this kiss would haunt him.

He mentally kicked himself on the way back to the motel. She was skittish again when it came to him. Distrustful.

He almost laughed at the thought. Hell, as it was, she didn't trust him as far as she could throw him. How could it be any worse?

But he knew the answer to that.

She could send him back to prison.

He was probably headed back there for another year, anyway. If she lost her job, which appeared likely, then this deal was over. He knew Stratton hadn't wanted him out to begin with, and with pressure from Shade Waters…

But that wasn't what worried him. It was Sheriff Claude McCray. McCray had seen the two of them together by the truck. He would make trouble for Jack. Dillon didn't doubt that for a second.

The tow truck driver finally arrived. Jack had been leaning against the side of the disabled pickup, arms crossed, a scowl on her face.

Dillon had had the good sense to leave her alone. Now he listened to Jack give the tow truck operator instructions to take the pickup to a tire shop, have the slashed tires replaced, the state billed, and the truck delivered to the motel in the morning.

The driver, a big burly guy with grease-stained fingers, grunted in answer before driving off with the pickup in tow.

"Pleasant fellow," Dillon commented as he and Jack were left alone in the dark parking lot.

She grunted in answer and started walking toward the motel. He guessed she needed the fresh air so he accompanied her and kept his mouth shut.

They hadn't gone a block, though, when her cell phone rang. She shot him a look. He felt his gut clench. It was the call they'd both been expecting all night. Once Stratton fired her, Dillon would be on his way back to Montana State Prison.

Well, at least he'd gotten a kiss, he told himself. And Chinese food. Sometimes that was as good as it got.

He could tell that Jack didn't want to talk to anyone, after everything that had happened tonight. As she checked her caller ID, he figured that, like him, she was worried it would be the sheriff.

"It's Stratton," she said, and gazed at

Dillon. They'd both been expecting this. He sure was calling late, though.

Was there some reason it had taken him so long? Maybe like he was giving it some consideration—until he got a call from the sheriff?

She snapped open the phone. "Wilde."

Dillon watched her face. A breeze stirred the hair around her face, and her eyes went wild, like those of a deer caught in headlights.

"I see." She listened for a while, then stated, "Fine. No, I understand. If that's what you want." She snapped the phone shut.

Dillon stared at her, trying to gauge the impact of the call. She looked strange, as if all evening she'd been preparing herself for the worst. Earlier, he'd had the feeling that she'd already given up the job. There'd been a freedom in her that had drawn him like a moth to a flame. "Well?"

"The rustlers hit again. Leroy Edmonds's ranch, to the east. Stratton thinks it was the same bunch. One of the ranch hands just found where the barbed wire fence was cut. Not sure when or how many head were stolen."

"Did Stratton…?"

"Fire me? No." She shook her head, as if this had been the last thing she'd expected. Maybe still couldn't believe it. "Waters apparently talked him out of it. Seems Waters has had a change of heart."

"Not likely," Dillon said with a curse, wondering what the bastard was up to.

Just as she had earlier, Jack looked to be close to tears. Tears of relief? Or just exhaustion? This day had to have played hell on her. He wished there was something he could do to make things easier for her. But he wasn't going to make the mistake of trying to kiss her again.

That woman at the steak house, the one who'd laughed and drank wine and seemed free, was gone. This one was all-business again.

"So you're telling me Waters has agreed to let us on his ranch?" Dillon asked, more than a little surprised.

"Sounds that way."

"Why the change of heart?" he had to ask.

"Shade says one of his ranch hands saw someone watching a grazing area with binoculars. He's agreed to let us talk to the hired hand and even have access to that section," she said. "That's a start."

She seemed relieved that she hadn't been

fired. But there was also a sadness about her. Dillon felt a stab of guilt for denigrating her job earlier.

"The sneaky son of a bitch," he said with a laugh. "He's that sure we won't catch him at whatever he's up to. Tell me this doesn't feel like a setup."

"I have to treat it like a legitimate lead," she said, sounding as if she wasn't any more happy about this than he was.

"I know. It's your job. But just do me one favor. No matter how sure you are that Waters is innocent, don't ever underestimate the bastard."

Jacklyn smiled. "Funny, that's what everyone keeps telling me about you."

Chapter Eleven

The next morning, with new tires on the truck, Jacklyn filled up the gas tank, then picked up the horse trailer and enough supplies to last a good three days.

"So we're headed for Leroy Edmonds's place?" Dillon asked, as Jack pointed the rig north again. "I thought you said his ranch was to the east?"

"First stop is Waters's spread. I need to talk to the hand who says he saw someone up in the hills scoping out the herd," she said.

He nodded, but sensed there was more going on with her this morning. Unless he was mistaken, there'd been a change in Jack. Not quite a twinkle in her eye, but close. He'd bet money she was up to something.

It was one of those blue-sky days that was so bright it was blinding. There wasn't a cloud in the sky and the weather was supposed to be good for nearly a week.

Dillon still couldn't believe he wasn't headed back to prison. It made him a little uneasy. "So who's the ranch hand?"

"Pete Barclay. He's worked for Waters ever since you went to prison," she said, glancing over at him.

She wasn't fooling him. All his old cowboy buddies were back in central Montana. Neither of them thought that was a coincidence.

He sighed deeply. "Pete Barclay."

"What? I thought Pete was your friend? Or are you going to tell me that he's now in cahoots with Waters?"

Dillon shook his head. There was no telling her anything. "Pete actually saw one of the rustlers?"

"The person was up in the hills. He saw a flash of light up in the rocks that he believes came from binocular lenses. When he went up to investigate, he found tracks. Look, I'm not sure what I believe at this point. That's why I want to talk to Pete."

"Right." There was more to it, sure as hell.

"If it makes you feel any better, I don't trust Waters," she admitted, as if the words were hard to say.

Dillon looked at her in surprise. That was the most honest she'd been with him. Not to mention that she'd just taken him into her confidence. Maybe he was finally making inroads with her. Or maybe she was just telling him what she thought he wanted to hear.

REDA HARPER HAD NEVER been good at letting sleeping dogs lie. She hadn't slept well last night, tossing and turning, her mind running over the meeting at the community center and, even more, what she'd seen on the W Bar.

She'd made a few calls first thing this morning to find out if the rustlers had struck again.

She'd been shocked to hear that, sure enough, they had hit another ranch. One to the east, though, not Waters's. How was that possible, when she'd have sworn she saw them on the W Bar last night? Unless she'd seen them *after* they'd hit Edmonds's ranch.

But what had she really seen?

"Isn't any of my business," she said to herself, even as she sat down at her desk and pulled out the pale lavender stationery. Caressingly, she ran her fingertips over the paper. Nicer than any paper she would have bought for herself. The stationery had been a gift from her lover.

"The no-good son of a bitch," she said under her breath. Her lips puckered, the taste in her mouth more sour than lemons as she picked up her pen and, with a careful hand, began to compose one of her infamous letters.

The mistake she'd made wasn't in mailing the letter, she realized later. It was in not leaving well enough alone and *only* sending the letter.

Even as she was pocketing shells and picking up her shotgun, she knew better. Not that she'd ever drawn the line at butting into other people's business. In fact, it was the only thing that gave her any satisfaction in her old age.

No, it was not leaving well enough alone when it came to Shade Waters. Her mother, bless her soul, had always said that Reda's anger would be the death of her.

Of course, her mother had never known about Reda's affair with Shade, so she'd never witnessed the true extent of her daughter's fury.

Had there been someone around to give Reda good advice, he or she would have told her not to get into her pickup armed with her shotgun. And maybe the best advice of all, not to go down that back road to where she'd seen that stock truck last night.

JACKLYN TURNED AT THE gate into the W Bar Ranch, taking a breath and letting it out slowly.

Last night she hadn't been able to sleep— not after the ranchers' meeting, everything she'd learned at the steak house with Dillon, and finally Stratton's call.

At least that's what she told herself. That it had been Dillon who gave her a sleepless night—and not just the kiss.

The night before had left her off balance. Even a little afraid. That wasn't like her, and she knew part of it was due to Dillon Savage. She'd known he was dangerous, but she'd underestimated his personality. Even his charm, she thought with a hidden smile.

But last night, unable to sleep, she'd realized what she had to do. As she drove into the W Bar, she knew the chance she was taking. She was no fool. She'd gotten Dillon out of prison for the reason he suspected: to give him enough rope that he would hang himself.

She'd been that sure he was the leader of the rustling ring.

Now she suspected that Stratton was doing the same thing with her.

This morning before they left, she'd called Shade Waters. He'd been almost apologetic. She'd questioned him why this was the first time she'd heard about one of his men seeing someone on the ranch. Why hadn't he mentioned it yesterday at his place? Or last night at the meeting?

"I just heard about it. I guess he told Nate and—" Waters let out a low curse "—Nate had other things on his mind and forgot to mention it until late last night."

"I want to talk to the ranch hand."

"I'll make sure he's here in the morning."

She'd wondered even then if Waters was making things too easy for her, setting her up, just as Dillon suspected. Or was she just letting Dillon sway her, the same way she'd let him kiss her last night?

As she parked in front of the ranch house, she was glad to see there wasn't a welcoming reception on the porch this time. "I need to talk to Pete alone."

"I'll be right here," Dillon said, lying back

and pulling his hat down over his eyes. He gave her a lazy grin.

"Make sure you stay here," she said.

He cut his eyes to her. They seemed bluer today than she'd ever seen them. Just a trick of the light. "At some point, you might want to give me more to do than sleep."

Soon, she thought. Very soon.

DILLON'S INTENTION had been to stay in the pickup. The last thing he wanted to do was make Jack mad again, he thought, as he watched her walk toward the barn. She did fill out her jeans nicely, he decided. He groaned, remembering the hard time he'd had getting to sleep last night, just thinking about their kiss.

He'd figured this early release would be a cakewalk. Just hang back, let things happen, do as little as he could. Jack was good at her job. She didn't need him.

But that had been before last night. Now he felt frustrated, on too many levels. He couldn't sit back and let Jack make the biggest mistake of her life.

The thought made him laugh. The biggest mistake of her life would be falling for him.

Yeah, like that was ever going to happen.

No, Jack was going at this all wrong. She was never going to catch the rustlers at this rate. She needed to investigate the W Bar and Waters.

Was she dragging her feet because of Dillon's own past with the rancher? He swore under his breath and sat up. The place was quiet. Maybe too quiet?

He told himself he had to think of what was best for him as well as Jack. She needed his help. He wondered how long it would be before he was headed back to prison, if she didn't get a break in this case.

Something shiny caught his eye. Grillwork on an old stock truck parked in tall weeds, behind what was left of a ramshackle older barn.

He thought of Jack for a moment. She'd disappeared into the new barn, closer to the house. He knew why she had balked at investigating Waters on the q.t. behind her supervisor's back. Because she didn't have a criminal mind.

But he did, he admitted with a grin, as he popped open his door and slipped out of the pickup. He wouldn't go far, but he definitely wanted to have a look at that truck. He was betting it was the same one he'd hitched a ride in just the day before.

Sneaking along the side of the building, Dillon kept an eye out for Jack. He hated to think what she would do if she caught him.

The W Bar definitely seemed too quiet as he neared the front of the truck. He hesitated at the edge of the building, flattening himself against the rough wood wall to listen. He could hear crickets chirping in the tall weeds nearby, smell dust on the breeze, mixed with the scents of hay and cattle, familiar smells that threatened to draw him back into that dark hole of his past.

After a moment, he inched around the corner of the barn and along the shady side the stock truck. It was cool here, wedged between the truck and the barn. He stayed low, just in case he wasn't alone. Strange that no one was around, other than the hired hand Jack was meeting with in the other barn. Pete Barclay, she'd said. He and Pete had never been close. Pete was a hothead.

That fact made Dillon nervous about Jack being in the barn alone with him. He reminded himself that she was wearing a gun, this was what she did for a living, and he had to trust her judgment.

Still, he was worried as he moved past the driver's door and along the wooden bed of the truck. He grabbed hold of one of the boards and climbed up the side, hesitating before he stuck his head over the top. He still hadn't heard any vehicles. No tractors. No ranch equipment. Not even the sound of a voice or the thunder of horses' hooves. Where was everyone?

As he finally peered over the top of the stock rack, Dillon wasn't all that surprised by what he found. The back of the truck had been washed out. There was only a hint of odor from the dead calves that had been in it yesterday.

Climbing down, he noticed that the truck was older than he'd realized yesterday. Probably why it was parked back here. Because it was seldom used.

He started around the corner of the barn, sensing too late that he was no longer alone.

JACKLYN FOUND Pete Barclay where Waters had told her he would be. In the barn. On her walk there, she saw no one else. She hadn't seen Waters's car, nor Nate's, for that matter, and suspected they might have gone into town to avoid her.

Which was fine with her.

Pete Barclay was a long, tall drink of water. He had a narrow face that she'd once heard called horsey, and he wore a ten-gallon Stetson that he was never going to grow into. His long legs were bowed, his clothing soiled, she noted, when she found him shoveling horse manure from the stalls.

"Mornin'," he said when he saw her, and kept on working.

"Shade told you I was coming out?"

Pete nodded.

"I just wanted to ask you a few questions."

"Sure." He shoveled the manure into a wheelbarrow, not looking at her.

"Shade said you saw someone watching the ranch?"

Pete dumped another shovelful into the wheelbarrow, the odor filling the air. Had Waters purposely told him to do this job this morning, because she would be talking to him?

"Can't say I saw anyone, just kind of a reflection. You know—like you get from binoculars."

"So you investigated?"

He nodded as he scooped up more manure. "Just found some boot and horseshoe prints. The ground was kind of trampled. Looked like someone had been hanging around behind a rock up there."

"And where was this, exactly?"

He told her. He still hadn't looked at her.

"Shade said you told Nate?"

He gave another nod.

"How many cattle would you say Mr. Waters has in that area?" she asked. She couldn't see Pete's face, but his neck flushed bright red.

"Mr. Waters said I wasn't to be giving out any numbers. Truth is he's talking about moving the cattle closer to the ranch house until the rustlers are caught."

"That's a good idea," she agreed, wondering if Shade had any idea what a terrible liar Pete was.

"He said to tell you to take the Old Mill Road. The country back in there is pretty rough. It's a good day's ride on horseback."

"Then I'd better get started," Jacklyn said.

SHADE WATERS STEPPED OUT in front of Dillon, blocking his way, as he came around the corner of the barn.

Dillon had often thought about what he would do if he ever caught the rancher in a dark alley, just the two of them alone, face-to-face.

"You and I need to talk," Waters said.

Dillon cocked his head, studying the man. Did the rancher have any idea how much danger he was in right now? Up close, Waters looked much older than he remembered him. He had aged, his skin sallow and flecked with sun spots. But there was still power in his broad frame. Shade Waters was still a man to be reckoned with.

"What could you and I possibly have to talk about?"

"Your father."

Dillon couldn't hide his surprise. He glanced toward the pickup, but didn't see Jack. "I don't think you want to go down that road."

"You're wrong about what happened," Waters said, sounding anxious. "I liked your father—"

"Don't," Dillon said, and pushed past the older man, striding toward the pickup, telling himself not to look back. His hands were shaking. It was all he could do not to turn around and go back and—

"I have a proposition for you," Waters said from behind him.

Dillon stopped walking. He took a deep breath and slowly turned.

"You want your father's ranch back? It's yours."

Dillon could only stare.

"I'll throw in the old Hanson place, as well."

Dillon took a step toward him, his fists clenched at his sides, anger making his head throb. "You think this will make up for the past?"

"I don't give a rat's behind about the past," Waters snapped. "This isn't a guilty gesture, for hell's sake. This is a business deal."

Dillon stopped a few yards from Waters. "Business?"

He couldn't believe this old fool. Waters had no idea the chance he was taking. In just two steps Dillon could finally get vengeance, if not justice.

"I give you the ranch, you take Morgan Landers off my hands," Waters said.

Dillon couldn't have been more astonished. "I beg your pardon? Off *your* hands?"

"Don't play dumb with me, Savage. What I always admired about you was your intelligence. You know damn well what I'm asking. I want her away from my son. Name your price."

Dillon shook his head, disbelieving. "My price?" he asked, closing the distance between them. This was the man who had destroyed his family, stolen his ranch and now thought he could buy him as well.

Dillon reached out and grabbed the man's

throat so quickly Waters didn't have a chance to react. He shoved the rancher against the side of the barn. "My price?"

"Dillon," Jacklyn said calmly, from behind him.

Waters's face had turned beet-red and he was making a choking sound.

"Dillon," Jacklyn repeated, still sounding calm and not overly concerned.

Dillon shot a look over his shoulder at her, saw her expression and let go of the rancher's throat.

Waters slumped against the side of the barn, gasping for air. "I'll have you back in prison for assault," he managed to wheeze as he clutched his throat.

"No, you won't," Dillon said to him quietly. "Or I'll tell your son what you just tried to do. Better yet, I'll tell Morgan."

Waters glared at him. "Get him the hell off my property," he growled to Jacklyn.

"We were just leaving," she said.

Next to her, Dillon walked toward the pickup, neither looking back.

"What was that about?" she asked under her breath, sounding furious.

"The bastard offered to give me back my ranch."

She shot him a look.

"And the old Hanson place thrown in."

"He admitted he'd stolen your ranch?" she said, once they were at the pickup and out of earshot.

"Yeah, right." Dillon glanced back. Waters was still standing beside the barn, glaring in their direction. "It was a business deal. He wanted me to take Morgan Landers off his hands."

As Jack opened her door, she glanced toward him in surprise. "You aren't serious."

"Dead-on," Dillon said as he joined her in the cab. He was still shaking, his heart pounding, at how close he'd come to going back to prison for good.

"He wants her out of his son's life that badly?"

Dillon laughed and leaned back in his seat as she started the engine and got rolling. "Waters is one manipulative son of a bitch. But I'd say he's met his match with Morgan Landers."

JACKLYN WATCHED Dillon's face as he glanced out in the direction of what had once been his family's ranch. "Tempted?" she asked.

He smiled but didn't look at her. "That train has already left the station."

She thought about the lovely Morgan Landers, heard the bitterness in his voice. Jacklyn had little doubt that Dillon could get the woman back if he wanted. Nate was no match for Dillon Savage.

"The sooner we catch these guys, the sooner you can get your life back," she said.

"What life?" He looked over at her and sighed. "I guess I do need to start thinking about the future."

She nodded. "Have you thought about what you want to do?"

"Sure." He looked out at the rolling grasslands they were passing. "I thought about leaving Montana, starting over."

"Using one of your degrees?"

He nodded, his expression solemn.

"But you can't leave here, can you?"

He turned to her again, then smiled slowly. "I don't think so."

But he couldn't stay here unless he let go of the past, and they both knew it.

Ahead, Jacklyn spotted the turnoff to the Old Mill Road. She slowed the truck. "You wouldn't have killed him."

Dillon laughed. "Don't bet the farm on it."

She shook her head. "You're not a killer, Dillon Savage."

He looked over at her and felt a rush of warmth that surprised him. Whether true or not, he liked that she seemed to believe it. He reminded himself that while she might not consider him capable of murder, she *did* believe he was behind the rustling ring. Or did she really?

Jacklyn turned down the road, amazed by the lengths Shade Waters would go to get what he wanted. Was it possible Dillon had been right about him all along?

The road was rutted and rough, and obviously didn't get much use. But clearly, a vehicle had been down here recently. There were fresh tire tread patterns visible in the dust.

As she topped a small rise, the huge old windmill, with only a few of the blades still intact, stood stark against the horizon. Near it, she spotted two vehicles parked in the shade of a grove of trees.

She swore under her breath as she recognized both of the people standing beside the vehicles, having what appeared to be an intimate conversation.

"And what do we have here?" Dillon said, as Sheriff McCray turned at the sound of the truck coming over the hill.

Jacklyn saw the sheriff's angry expression. He left Morgan and walked over to stand in the middle of the road, blocking it.

"Tempted?" Dillon said with amusement when Jacklyn brought the pickup to a stop just inches from McCray's chest.

With a groan, she powered down her window as the sheriff walked around to her side of the vehicle. He didn't look happy to see her. Or was it that he wasn't happy to be caught out here with Morgan?

"What are you doing here?" McCray demanded, glancing from her to Dillon. "You spying on me?" Clearly, he was upset at being caught. But caught doing what?

She glanced toward Morgan, who had gotten into her SUV and was now leaving. "Shade said one of his men noticed someone watching this end of the ranch. I told him I'd check it out."

McCray frowned. "Why would he tell you that? There's no cattle in here." His eyes narrowed. "You're going to have to come up with a better story than that."

No she wasn't. "My mistake." She shifted the pickup into Reverse and, backing up the horse trailer into a low spot, turned around.

But McCray wasn't done with her. He stepped up to her window. "Or maybe you had another reason for coming out here," he said, scowling at Dillon.

"I could ask what *you* are doing out here," Jacklyn snapped, before she could stop herself.

"I'm doing my job," he retorted defensively. "Shade asked me to keep an eye on his place."

"Really?" She glanced toward the retreating Morgan Landers. "Or did he make you an offer you couldn't refuse?" Claude ignored that.

"I see you got yourself some new tires," he said with snide satisfaction, no doubt to let her know he'd seen Dillon kissing her last night in the community center parking lot.

"Don't let me keep you from your…*work*," she said as she let the clutch out a little quicker than she'd planned. The pickup lurched forward, the tire almost running over the sheriff's foot.

He jumped back with a curse. As she turned the wheel and left, she saw him in her rearview mirror, mouthing something at her. She gave the pickup more gas and heard Dillon chuckle.

"I wonder what Waters offered *him?*"

Dillon said. "That looked like a lovers' tryst to me. I just hope I'm around when Morgan finds out that Shade Waters is trying to sell her to anyone who'll take her."

As Jacklyn drove back the way they'd come, she only momentarily wondered just how far Shade would go to protect his son from Morgan Landers—and what Nate would do if he found out.

But her mind was on what McCray had said about Waters not running any cattle in that section of the ranch. She'd known Pete Barclay was lying, but now she knew that Waters was, as well.

Chapter Twelve

As Jacklyn reached the county road, a truck whizzed past, headed in the direction of the W Bar Ranch.

"That's odd," she said, as she caught a glimpse of the man behind the wheel. Buford Cole had to have seen them, but appeared to turn away, as if not wanting to be recognized.

"Looks like he's headed for Waters's ranch," Dillon said, lifting a brow.

She was reminded of what Buford had told her at the steak house. "He's a friend of yours." She hadn't meant to make it sound so much like an accusation.

Dillon looked away. "I lost some friends when I went to prison. Buford was one of them."

That surprised her. "Why was that?"

He turned to smile at her. "You tell me.

Was he the one who helped you capture me? I've always wondered who betrayed me."

She heard the pain in his voice. But it was the underlying anger that worried her. "No one helped me."

He gave her a look that said he didn't believe that for a minute.

"Buford used to rustle cattle with you, didn't he?"

Dillon didn't reply. But then, she thought she knew the answer. Buford had known too much about Dillon's motives not to have helped him.

And what about Dillon's other buddies, Pete Barclay and Arlen Dubois? Dillon hadn't seemed happy to see any of them. And now that she thought about it, they were giving him distance, as well. Because they didn't want her to know that they were still involved in rustling together?

"If I were you, I wouldn't trust anything Buford told you," Dillon said finally.

"Why?"

He looked at her as if she wasn't as smart as he'd thought. "Because he can't be trusted."

"Unlike you. Is Buford smart enough to be running this latest rustling gang?"

Dillon shook his head without hesitation. "He's smart enough, but he has no imagination."

"Rustling requires imagination?" she asked, half-mockingly.

He grinned. "As a matter of fact, it does. Whoever is running this gang has imagination. Look what they pulled off at the Crowleys'. Stealing the cattle in broad daylight right in front of the house. That took imagination. And bravado."

She heard admiration in his voice.

"Don't be giving me that look," he said. "If I was the one behind this gang, do you think I'd be bragging on myself?"

"As a matter of fact…."

DILLON GLANCED UP as she pulled off the road. Out the windshield, all he could see was pasture beyond the barbed wire fence gate. He shot Jack a questioning look. She appeared to be waiting for him to get out and open a gate that hadn't been opened for some time. The fence posts on both sides were clearly marked with orange paint.

In Montana any fool knew that a fence post painted orange meant no trespassing. It meant prosecution under the law if caught on that land. And up here, especially with a band of rustlers on the loose, the rancher would be prone to shoot first and ask questions later.

Especially this rancher, because the land on the other side of that gate was W Bar property, belonging to Shade Waters.

"What the hell?" Dillon asked quietly as he met her gaze.

"I called Stratton this morning and told him we would be going north up by the Milk River for a few days, to follow a lead," she said.

Dillon felt an odd ache in his chest. She'd lied to her boss, just as he'd suggested she should do. "Are you sure about this?"

"No," she said without hesitation. "If you want to know the truth, I suspect you're setting me up. But Waters lied about having cattle down by the old windmill and Pete lied about seeing someone in that area. I can only assume Shade was just trying to keep me busy. And that makes me wonder if he isn't trying to keep me away from another part of his ranch. You said that stock truck was headed north, right?"

Dillon nodded slowly.

"Toward your old ranch."

"Looked that way."

"Any thoughts on why he would get rid of the rustled calves on your family's old place?"

Dillon smiled at that. "For the same reason you're thinking. To make it look like I had something to do with it."

She nodded.

"So when I told you about the calves in the back of the stock truck, you *believed* me?" he asked.

"I wouldn't go that far. I wanted to do a little investigating on my own first." She reached into the glove box, pulled out a map and spread it on the seat between them. "Okay, Waters ranch house is here. Most of his cattle are in this area." She looked up at Dillon. "I had a friend who owns a plane fly over it early this morning."

He met her gaze. "You are just full of surprises."

"The problem is there's no way to get to your old ranch anymore without driving right past Waters's house." She pointed to the map. "Reda Harper's place is past his. According to the map, there used to be a section road that connected with another county road to the east, but that's now part of the W Bar."

"Waters closed the road after he bought our ranch," Dillon said, trying to keep the emotion out of his voice. Waters had had his family's ranch house razed.

"Can I ask you something?"

Her tone as much as her words surprised him. And he knew before she asked that her question wasn't about cattle rustling business.

"This bad blood between you and Shade Waters, am I wrong in suspecting it goes deeper than his ending up with your ranch?" she asked.

Dillon chuckled and looked toward the mountains in the distance. "I told you Nate had an older brother. He was killed trying to ride a wild horse." His voice sounded flat over the painful beating of his heart. "Halsey was my best friend." He looked at her. "It happened on our ranch."

She let out a breath as if she'd been holding it, compassion and understanding in her eyes. "Shade blamed you."

He nodded. "And my family. Halsey was…" He chewed at his cheek for a moment. "Well, there just wasn't anyone like him. A day hasn't gone by that I haven't missed him."

"It must be worse for Shade," she said.

"Halsey was definitely his favorite of the two boys." Dillon looked down at the map. "So what we need is a way to get to my old ranch without Waters or his men seeing us, right?" he asked, hoping she'd let him change the subject.

"Right," she said, to his relief. "I thought you might have some ideas."

He managed a grin. "You know me. I'm just full of good ideas."

"Let's see if we can find those calves," Jack said. "Open the gate, Mr. Savage. You're about to get us both arrested for trespassing."

JACKLYN WOUND HER WAY among rocks and sage, across open grasslands. As soon as she reached a low spot where she was sure the truck and horse trailer couldn't be seen from the county road, she cut the engine.

The former Savage Ranch land was miles away, but the only way to get there without being seen was by horseback. Water and wind had eroded the earth to the north, carving canyons and deep ravines that eventually spilled into the Missouri River. It was badlands, inaccessible by anything but horseback, and isolated. They would have a long ride. That's why she'd brought provisions in case they had to camp tonight.

Jacklyn didn't doubt for an instant that Waters would have them arrested for trespassing if he caught them before they could find the evidence they needed to open up an investigation.

"You suspected the calves are buried on my family's former ranch the minute I told you about the dead calves, didn't you?" Dillon said with a grin as they saddled up their horses and loaded supplies into the saddlebags.

She just smiled at him. The truth was she'd had a hard time believing his story. Why kill the calves? What was the point of rustling them in the first place?

But the more she'd pondered the topic, the more she couldn't help thinking about what Dillon had said regarding motive. Was there a chance it had nothing to do with money? That the rustlers didn't want the calves—they just wanted them stolen?

It made no sense to her, but it seemed to make sense to Dillon. If what Buford had told her was true, Dillon had rustled cattle as retribution against his neighboring ranchers and Waters. He hadn't wanted the cattle, either.

Which made her suspicious, given that the current rustlers appeared to have a similar, nonmonetary motive.

"Don't you wonder why the rustled calves

are being dumped on my former land?" Dillon asked.

"Like you said, it makes you look guilty."

"But you know I'm too smart for that," he said, grinning at her.

Again Jack smiled back. "Right. You're so smart you would have the rustled cattle put on your land to frame Waters, by making it look like he was trying to frame you."

Dillon laughed, shaking his head.

But the truth was he looked worried. And maybe with good reason. If DNA tests were run on the dead calves he'd seen, she'd bet it would match cattle stolen from the same ranches that he had stolen from in the past.

"What if you never get justice?" she asked seriously.

Dillon seemed surprised by her question. "Isn't that the reason you do the job you do? To make sure justice is served?" He winked at her. "See, you and I aren't that different after all, Jack. We just have our own way of getting the job done."

She watched Dillon ride on ahead of her. He looked at home in the saddle. She'd come to realize there was little Dillon Savage wasn't capable of doing. Or willing to do for justice. Was that why he was helping her now?

As if he felt her eyes on him, he slowed his horse, turning to look back at her. Their gazes locked for a moment. He smiled as if he knew that she'd been studying him.

She looked away, hating that he made her heart beat a little faster. Worse, that he knew it. Dillon Savage was arrogant enough without seeing any kind of interest in her eyes.

"Everything all right?" he asked, reining in his horse to ride next to her again.

"Fine."

His grin broadened. "You don't have to always play the tough guy."

"Who's playing?"

He laughed. "You know, Jack, I like you. I don't care what other people say about you."

It was an old joke, but it still made her smile. Maybe because she knew at least the part about other people was true.

"Some men may hold a grudge toward you," he said as he rode alongside her. "But you and I understand each other."

She glanced at him, wondering if that was true.

SHADE WATERS STOOD at the front window, watching his son's SUV barrel up the road. Nate hadn't come home last night. Where had he been? Shade could only guess. He'd been with Morgan Landers.

Waters waited anxiously, having made a decision. He had to tell Nate exactly what would happen if he persisted in dating this woman.

As the car came to a stop, Shade saw that Nate wasn't alone, and swore. Morgan. Well, he'd have one of the ranch hands take her back to town, because he couldn't put off this talk with his son. He wouldn't.

Waters didn't turn at the sound of footfalls on the porch or the opening and closing of the door. He realized he was shaking, his entire body trembling.

"Nate." He cleared his voice, raising it. "Nate. I need to talk to you. Alone."

He finally turned as Nate entered the room. His son looked like hell. Obviously hungover, as if he'd pulled an all-nighter. Waters felt disgust as he stared at his youngest offspring. If only his elder son, Halsey, had lived.

"Dad…" Nate said, and Morgan appeared at his side, looping her arm through his, a big, victorious smile on her face.

Shade felt his heart drop. "I want to speak to my son alone." He saw Morgan give a little tug on Nate's arm.

"Dad," Nate began again. "There's something I need to tell you." He didn't sound happy about it. Or was he just afraid of Shade's reaction? "Morgan and I got married last night."

Shade felt the floor beneath him threaten to crumble to dust. He watched his every dream fly out the window. He'd always hoped that Nate would change, that he'd grow up and want to take the ranch to the next level. He'd hoped Nate would make the Waters name known not only all across Montana, but also the Northwest. Maybe even farther. Anything would have been possible.

But as he looked at his son's hangdog face, Shade knew that Nate would only run the ranch into the ground. And Morgan... He looked at her self-satisfied expression and knew she would bleed the place dry, then dump Nate for someone with more to offer.

He saw every dream he'd ever had for the W Bar disappear before his eyes.

"Congratulations," he said, hoping the break in his voice didn't give him away. He stepped to his son and shook his hand, squeezing a little too hard.

Then he kissed Morgan on the cheek, embracing her, even smiling. Both newlyweds were surprised and taken aback. They'd run off to get married, afraid he'd try to stop them. Now they expected him to be upset, even to rant and rave and threaten them.

Clearly, neither knew him very well.

"I wish you both the best," he said, almost meaning it. "This calls for champagne. You will join me for dinner tonight, won't you?"

They both readily agreed, and Waters smiled to himself.

He'd break the news at dinner.

JACKLYN RODE THE HORSE across sun-drenched, rolling hills miles from the nearest road, the grasses vibrant green, the air sharp with the scents of spring. Dillon rode next to her, his gaze more often than not on the horizon ahead—on land that had once been in his family for five generations.

For a long time, neither spoke. She could see how much Dillon was enjoying this. There was a freedom about him even though she had the tracking monitor in her saddlebag.

They stopped for lunch in a stand of trees, letting their horses graze while they ate their sandwiches. Out here, Jacklyn felt as if she was a million miles from civilization.

After lunch, they rode on again, across land starting to change from prairie to badlands.

"So tell me about your childhood," Dillon said out of the blue once they were back in the saddle. "Come on, Jack, we've got a long ride today. If you don't want me to sing—and believe me, you don't—then talk to me. You a Montana girl or a transplant?" When she didn't answer, he said, "Okay, if you want me to guess—"

"Montana. I grew up around West Yellowstone. I was an only child. My mother taught school. My father was a game warden."

Dillon let out a low whistle. "That explains a lot. Now I see where you get it."

"The game warden father," she said sarcastically.

"No, the schoolteacher mother," he joked, and she had to smile. "See? That wasn't so hard."

"So tell me about you," she said.

"Come on, Jack, you know my whole life story. What you didn't already know I'm sure Buford Cole filled you in on the other night at the steak house."

She couldn't hide her surprise.

He grinned. "Yeah, I saw him talking to you. I can just imagine what he had to say."

"Can you? He said you're a man who holds a grudge."

His grin broadened. "Buford should know. We're cut from the same cloth."

"He also said he wouldn't be surprised if you were leading this gang of rustlers."

Dillon laughed. "You don't believe that anymore," he said as he rode on ahead.

When she caught up to him, Dillon could tell she had something on her mind. "Come on, let's have it," he said.

"I was just thinking how different you are from your cousin Hud."

Oh boy, here it comes. As if he hadn't heard that his whole life. "How is Hud?" he asked, although he knew.

"He married his childhood sweetheart, Dana Cardwell. She owns a ranch in the Gallatin Canyon."

Dillon nodded. He liked her voice, her facial expressions when she spoke. "I heard something about a lost will," he said, encouraging her.

"Dana's mother had told her she made up a new will leaving the ranch to her, with some of the income divided among the siblings, along with some other assets. For a while Dana couldn't find the document leaving her the ranch, and it looked like she would have to sell to settle with her sister and brothers."

"But the ranch was saved," Dillon said, hating the bitterness he heard in his voice.

Unfortunately, Jack heard it, too. "Weren't you away when your father sold the family ranch?"

He gave her a self-deprecating grin. "You know I was. But then, like I said, you know everything about me. You probably know when I had my first kiss, my first—"

"I know it is hard to lose something you love," she said quickly, to cut him off, no doubt afraid of where he was headed.

"Have you ever lost something you loved?" he asked, studying her.

"Dana's pregnant." Jack looked away as she changed the subject. "She and Hud are expecting their first child this fall."

That surprised Dillon. He hadn't seen his cousin in years. But Uncle Brick had stopped up to the prison a few times a year to give Dillon a lecture and tell him how glad he was that his brother and sister-in-law weren't still alive to see their son behind bars. Brick had also shared the going-ons with the family. The pregnancy must have been a recent development.

"I'm happy for Hud and Dana," Dillon said, meaning it. "A baby." Hud would make a great father. For the first time, Dillon felt a prickle of envy. Hud with a wife and a baby and living on Dana's family ranch.

Settling down had been the last thing Dillon had imagined doing. He'd always told himself he would be bored to death with that kind of life. He needed excitement, adventure, challenge.

Hell, apparently he needed to be running from the law.

"If you don't buy a ranch in the future, what will you do?" she asked.

He'd had plenty of time to think about what he would do once he was really free. "Can you see me behind a desk, wearing a three-piece suit?"

"Yes."

He laughed. "Liar." This felt good between them. Lighter. Freer. He liked it. He liked her, in spite of everything. That surprised him.

"So I guess you'll ranch, since apparently cattle are in your blood."

"Raising cattle so someone can steal them?" He chuckled to hide how close she'd come to the truth. "But then, you'd be around to catch the rustlers, right?"

She looked away.

"Hey, don't worry about me," he said, moving into her range of vision to smile at her.

"I'd hate to see you go back to rustling," she said quietly.

"I'm sure you're aware that my grandfather left me money," Dillon said. "It's not like I need to find a job."

"Everyone needs a job," she said adamantly. "You need something to occupy your mind. Especially *your* mind."

I have something to occupy my mind, he thought as he looked at her.

"How much farther?" she asked, as if feeling the heat of his gaze.

"I think I know where the calves are buried and how to get there." Dillon had been trying to think like Shade Waters. He regretted to realize that it wasn't that hard. He'd gotten to know the man too well. Maybe had even become too much like him over the years.

"On the other side of the canyon," he said. He'd been mulling over why Waters would be rustling cattle. It made no sense. Especially just to kill them. Was he trying to force out ranchers in the county so he could buy their land like he had Dillon's father?

The W Bar was so huge now that Waters

had to be having trouble running it all. Dillon doubted Nate was of any help. Nate had never been much of a cowboy, let alone a rancher. Unlike his brother, Halsey, who had loved ranch life as much as Dillon had.

Also what didn't make sense—if he was right and Waters was dumping some of the stolen cattle on the old Savage Ranch—was why? Sure, he and the big rancher couldn't stand the sight of each other, but Dillon was small potatoes. Waters was too smart to risk everything to try to get even with Dillon after all this time. And hadn't he just offered to give back the ranch if Dillon got Morgan out of his life?

But what really worried him was why Buford Cole would be going to the W Bar. Buford had hated Waters as much as Dillon did. Or at least Dillon had thought so.

Ahead, the rolling prairie rose to rocky bluffs. "The canyon will be hot, but the route is shorter this way."

She glanced over at him. Was that suspicion he saw in her eyes?

"It isn't like we've been followed," he said, looking over his shoulder. He could see for miles. No one knew they were here. And yet he couldn't shake the feeling that Waters was one step ahead of them, laying a trap they were about to walk into.

As they rode between the rocks and into the narrow canyon, rocks and trees towering on each side, Dillon felt even more unease.

"Just a minute," he said, reaching out to touch Jack's hand on the reins.

She brought her horse up. "What's wrong?"

He wished he knew what to tell her. How could he explain this feeling? "Let me go first," he said, adding, "I know the way."

The look she gave him said she doubted there was a chance of getting lost in the narrow canyon, but she let him ride ahead of her.

He urged his horse among the rocks. There was no breeze in here, only heat. It felt stifling. That and quiet. He was regretting coming this way when a shadow fell over him.

He glanced up in time to see a hawk soar low over the rocks, its shadow flickering over the canyon for a few seconds before it was gone.

Dillon was literally jumping at shadows. What the hell was wrong with him?

As he turned to look back at Jack, he felt his horse stumble and heard a metal ping like the snapping of a guitar string.

"Get back!" he yelled, and jerked his

mount's head around, digging his boot heels into its flanks.

He grabbed her reins as his horse rushed past hers, pulling her with him as the first rocks began to fall.

Their horses bounded along the canyon floor as the air filled with dust and the roar of a rockslide.

Chapter Thirteen

Jacklyn bent over her horse as Dillon charged ahead on his, drawing her after him through the tight canyon.

Behind her she could hear the crash of rocks. Dust filled the air, obliterating everything. Then, suddenly, they were riding out of the dust, out of the canyon. The breeze chilled her skin as Dillon brought the horses to a stop in the open.

"Are you all right?" he cried, swinging around to look at her.

She nodded. "What was that back there?" she demanded, knowing it was no accident.

"A booby trap."

She stared at him, not comprehending. "You're telling me someone was waiting for us in the canyon? How is that possible? No one knew we were headed this way."

"The booby trap was wired to set off the

rockslide if anyone tried to come up through the canyon."

"Who would do such a thing?"

Dillon gave her a knowing look. "Who do you think?"

"You aren't going to try to tell me that Shade Waters rigged that, are you?"

He gave her a cold stare. "No. I doubt he knows how."

She felt a chill. "But you do." She remembered six years ago almost getting caught in a rockslide when she was chasing him.

"Oh, my God," she said, drawing back from him.

"The difference is that mine was just to slow you down," he said. "There was no chance of you being hurt."

She shook her head, wondering if she would ever really know this man. It was an odd thought, since more than likely he would be going back to prison. Where he belonged.

"I never did it again," he said, his gaze holding hers. "Too many things can go wrong. I didn't want your death on my conscience."

She realized she was still trembling inside at their near tragedy as she glanced back up the canyon. "You know who rigged that, don't you," she said quietly.

"No, but I used to know some men who were acquainted with the technique."

She turned in her saddle to look at him. "You're talking about the men who rode with you. I've never understood why you didn't give up their names. You could have gotten less time in prison if you had."

"Don't you know me better than that?" With a shake of his head, he added, "I made a lot of mistakes before I went to prison."

"You mean like getting caught."

He locked eyes with her, his expression intense even though he was smiling. "No, before that. I started off with what I felt was a damn good reason for what I did. But if prison taught me anything, it was that, while vindicated, I lost more than my freedom. I'm trying to get that back."

"What do we do now?" she asked, glancing at her watch. They had been riding most of the day. They were losing light.

"We'll have to go around the bluffs. It will take longer, but it will be safer."

"You expect other booby traps?"

"No. But I'm not taking any chances. The

good news is that the rockslide confirmed what we suspected. They had to have gotten rid of the stolen calves on the other side of the canyon. That's why they booby-trapped it from this side."

"Either that or they were expecting us because they know you," she said.

Dillon's eyes narrowed as he looked toward the canyon. "Yeah, that's another possibility, isn't it?"

THE SUN HAD MADE its trip from horizon to horizon by the time they reached the other side of the canyon. The shadows of the bluffs ran long and dark. The air had cooled. They still had a couple of hours of daylight. Jacklyn hoped they'd find the evidence, then ride out to the road, and avoid being forced to camp tonight.

She'd made sure they had the supplies they needed, just in case. There was no telling how long it would take to find where the calves had been buried. She refused to consider the possibility that Dillon was wrong, that Waters had too much land to hide in, that it might be impossible to find the dead calves—let alone that they didn't exist, that she'd been taken in by Dillon.

She concentrated her thoughts on Shade Waters. As arrogant as the man was, he would feel safe, if he was behind the rustling. This part of the ranch was isolated, far from a public road and all his land. He would feel confident doing whatever he wanted back here, she told herself. No matter what happened in this remote section, no one would be the wiser.

And there would be some poetic justice in dumping the cows on what had been the Savage Ranch.

At the top of a hill, Dillon reined in his horse. She joined him, glad to see that they'd finally made it to the old section road. Jacklyn could make out the hint of tracks, faint as a memory, through the grass.

"They left us a trail," Dillon said.

From this point, they could see for miles to the west. Almost as far as Waters's ranch house, but not quite. The good news was there were no vehicles in sight.

They rode down the hill and followed the faint tracks through the deep grass along what had once been a section road between the Savage and Waters ranches. Someone had definitely been using it lately.

There had been a barbed wire fence along

both sides of the road, but Waters had it taken down after he'd bought out Dillon's father.

Jacklyn could feel the change that came over Dillon. The land off to their left had once been his. He would have probably been ranching it now if not for Waters.

She saw him looking ahead to the rocky bluffs, and wished she'd known him before he became a cattle thief.

"There's been more than one rig on this road," Dillon said.

"Can you still get out this way?" she asked, thinking that the road must dead-end a few miles from here.

"You can reach the county road, if you know where you're going," he said, pointing to the southeast.

The road wound through the badlands. To the right ahead was the opening to the canyon they'd tried to come up. To the left were more deep ravines and towering bluffs, then miles of ranch land.

As they rode closer to the canyon entrance, she saw the distinct track through the grass where someone had driven off the road back into the rocks. She could hear a meadowlark's sweet song, feel the day slipping away as the air cooled around her and the light dimmed.

She felt an urgency suddenly and rode out ahead, following the tracks. Along with the urgency was an overwhelming sense of dread. How many cattle had been buried back here? She hated to think.

She reined in in surprise where one set of vehicle tracks veered off to the left, while the other headed to the right, toward the canyon entrance.

As Dillon joined her, he reached over and touched her shoulder. "Look," he said, his voice a low, worried murmur.

She followed his gaze to a rock outcropping and saw the glint of light off a windshield. Her gaze met his as she unsnapped the holster on her weapon. Sliding off her horse to the ground, she whispered, "Wait here."

"Not a chance," he whispered back.

Ground-tying her horse, Jacklyn moved cautiously toward the vehicle hidden among the rocks. Dillon walked next to her, as quietly as a cat. The air that had felt cool and smelled sweet just moments before became stifling as she entered the shadow of the bluffs. Crickets chirped from the nearby grass, overhead a hawk cried out as it soared in a wide circle, and yet there was a deathly quiet that permeated the afternoon.

"IT'S REDA HARPER'S pickup," Jack said as they rounded the rocks and saw where someone had hidden the truck.

Dillon peered inside. Empty. "You don't think Reda is behind the rustling, do you?"

Jack shrugged. She wouldn't have put anything past the ranchwoman, even rustling cattle. "You have to admit she's smart enough to be the leader of the rustling ring. Otherwise, what is her truck doing here?" She glanced up as if the words had just hit her, and shook her head, dread in every line of her face.

"I'll go have a look, and if everything checks out—"

"Not a chance," she said, echoing his words. "I got you into this. I won't be responsible for you getting killed while I stand by."

He smiled at that. "Be careful," he said softly. "You're going to make me think you're starting to like me."

"Don't you wish," she joked as she strode toward her horse.

Yeah, he did wish, he thought as he watched her swing into the saddle. He reminded himself that this was the woman who'd captured him and helped send him to prison. But the memory didn't carry the usual sting. He smiled to himself as he caught his reins and swung up onto his horse. He was starting to like her. More than he should.

"I forgot that you see me only as a means to an end," he said as he looked at her. "I need to keep reminding myself of that."

She didn't glance at him, but he saw color heat her throat. Had he hit a little close to home or had their relationship changed since she'd gotten him out of prison?

He told himself, as he led the way, that he must be crazy if he thought he might be getting to Jack. True, she wasn't calling him Mr. Savage anymore. She was still ordering him around, but he wasn't paying any attention. And she hadn't sent him back to prison even though they hadn't caught the rustlers. Yet.

All in all, he hadn't made much progress with her. But then, he supposed that depended on what kind of progress he wanted to make. His plans had changed, he realized. He no longer felt any anger toward her. If only he felt the same way about Shade Waters…

The canyon was wider at this end. A few aspens grew in clumps along the sides of the bluffs, their leaves whispering in the breeze as he and Jack rode past.

They hadn't gone far, following the tire tracks in the soft earth, when he spotted the backhoe and the freshly turned earth a dozen yards down a small ravine at one side of the canyon. That the rustlers had used a backhoe to bury the calves didn't surprise him.

It was the pile of rocks that had cascaded down from the canyon wall along one side of the ravine that brought him up short. He let out a curse as Jack rode ahead of him, dismounting near the tumbled heap.

He went after her, already pretty sure he knew what she was about to find when he saw the shotgun lying to one side.

She let out a small cry and dropped to her knees beside the pile. The fallen rocks were shot with color.

"Jack, don't!" Dillon yelled as she frantically began throwing stones to one side. "It's too late."

JACKLYN DIDN'T REMEMBER dismounting and rushing to the rocks. Didn't remember falling to her knees beside the pile or reaching out to touch the bright fabric of a shirtsleeve.

All the time, she must have known what

was trapped underneath, but it wasn't until she moved one of the rocks and saw first a hand, the nails short but bright red with polish, then a face contorted in pain and death, that she let out a cry and stumbled back.

Dillon grabbed her, pulling her to him. "There's nothing you can do. She's dead."

Jacklyn pressed her face against his chest, his shirt warm, his chest solid. She needed solidity right now. In her line of work, she took chances. She carried a gun. She knew how to shoot it, but she'd never had to use it. Nor was she in the habit of finding dead bodies. Cows, yes. People, no.

She just needed a moment to catch her breath, to get her emotions under control, to stop shaking. That's all it took. A moment listening to Dillon's steady heartbeat, feeling his arms wrapped protectively around her. She stepped back, nodding her thanks, under control again even if she was still shaking inside.

"We have to call someone," she said, as she dug out her cell phone.

Dillon watched, looking skeptical. "I doubt you'll be able to get service—"

She swore. "No service."

He nodded.

She glanced at the pile of rocks, then quickly turned her head away. "What was she doing here? She must have seen the backhoe in here and walked back to investigate."

Dillon shook his head. "What was she doing on Waters's ranch to begin with?"

That was the question, wasn't it. Everyone in the county knew there was no love lost between the two of them.

"I need to see if I can get the phone to work higher up in the hills," Jacklyn said, reaching for her horse's reins so she could swing up into the saddle. "I'll ride up—" She heard Dillon call out a warning, but it was too late.

She was already spinning her horse around, only half in the saddle, headed for a high spot on the bluffs, when she heard a sound that chilled her to the bone.

SHADE WATERS LOOKED UP from his plate in the middle of dinner and realized he hadn't been listening. He'd insisted they eat early because he had some things to take care of.

"Shade," Morgan said in that soft, phony Southern drawl of hers. "I asked what you thought about my idea."

"What idea is that, Morgan?"

"Redecorating the house. It's so…male. And so…old-fashioned. Don't you think it's time for some changes around here?"

He could well imagine the changes she really meant. "Definitely," he said. "In fact, that's what I was doing, thinking it was high time for some changes around here."

Morgan looked a little surprised. He was taking this all too well. He knew she kept wondering why he wasn't putting up a fight.

"My first suggestion," he said, looking over at his son, "is that you both move into town."

Nate started in surprise. "What?"

"I'm changing my will in the morning," Shade announced. "I'm not going to leave you a dime. Oh, I know you'll spend years fighting it, but I can assure you, the way I plan to change my will, you'll lose. You'll never have the W Bar," he said, his gaze going to Morgan. "Or any of my money."

For once Morgan appeared speechless.

"Dad, you can't—"

"Oh, Nate, I can. And I will. You have no interest in the ranch. You never have. As for your…*wife*—"

"I think your father might be getting senile," Morgan said, glaring at Shade. "Clearly he is no longer capable of making such an important decision."

The rancher laughed. "I wondered how long it would take before you'd try to have me declared incompetent. Understand something, both of you. I will burn this place to the ground, lock, stock and barrel, before either of you will ever have it." He tossed down his napkin. "I have an appointment with my lawyer in the morning. I suggest you find a nice apartment in town to redecorate, Mrs. Waters. And Nate, you might want to find a job."

With that, he left the room, doing his best not to let them see that his legs barely held him up and he was shaking like the leaves on an aspen. The moment he was out of the house, he slumped against the barn wall and fought to control his trembling as he wiped sweat from his face with his sleeve.

He'd done it. There was no turning back now.

JACKLYN'S HORSE SHIED an instant after she heard the ominous rattle. Both caught her by surprise. She only had one foot in a stirrup as the animal reared. The next thing she knew she was falling backward, her boot caught there.

"Jack!" she heard Dillon yell as he lunged for her and her horse.

She hit the ground hard and felt pain shoot through her ankle as it twisted. Her horse shied to the side, dragging her with it, the pain making everything go black, then gray.

When her vision cleared she saw Dillon leap from his horse and grab her mount's reins, dragging the mare to a stop before he gently freed Jacklyn's boot from the stirrup.

She would have cried out in pain, but the fall had knocked the air from her lungs. She lay in the dust, unable to breathe, the throbbing in her ankle so excruciating it took her a moment to realize the real trouble she was in.

Out of the corner of her eye, she saw the rattlesnake coiled not a foot from her. The snake's primeval head was raised, tongue protruding, beaded eyes focused on her as its tail rattled loudly, a blur of movement and noise as it lunged at her face.

The air filled with a loud boom that made her flinch.

The snake jerked. Blood splattered on the rocks behind it, then the serpent lay still.

In that split second before she saw the rattler lunge at her, and heard the deafening report of the gun, Jacklyn had seen her life pass before her eyes, leaving her with only one regret.

The boom of her gun startled her into taking a breath. She gasped, shaken, the pain in her ankle making the rest of her body feel numb and disconnected.

Dillon dropped to the ground next to her, her gun still in his hand. Later, she would recall the brush of his fingers at her hip in that instant before the snake struck.

She took deep ragged breaths, eyes burning with tears of pain and relief and leftover fear.

"How badly are you hurt?" Dillon asked as he looked into her beautiful face. There was no doubt that she was hurting, even though she tried to hold back the tears. Her body was trembling, but he couldn't tell if it was from pain or fright.

"I'm fine," she managed to say, lying through her teeth. He could see that she was far from fine. But he let her try to get to her feet, ready to catch her when she gave a cry of pain and was forced to sit back down.

He handed her the gun. "Let's try my question again. How badly are you hurt?"

"It's my ankle," she said, replacing the pistol in her holster with trembling fingers.

"Let me take a look." He gently urged her

to lie down, watching her face as he carefully eased her jeans up her leg. "I don't want to take off the boot yet." She wouldn't be able to ride without it. Also, it would keep the swelling down.

As he carefully worked his way down one side of her boot with his warm fingers, tears filled her eyes. She tried to blink them back and couldn't.

"I don't think it's broken. But if it's not, it's one nasty sprain." He looked past her and saw that both horses had taken off, skittish over the rattlesnake or the gun blast.

"I need to go round up the horses. Will you be all right for a few minutes?"

"Of course."

He nodded, glancing around to make sure there were no more rattlers nearby. "I'll be right back."

"Take your time. I'm fine."

He rose to his feet, then leaned back down. "Do not try to walk on that ankle. You'll only make matters worse if you do."

"I'm aware of that." She sounded as if she would have cried if he hadn't been there.

THE MOMENT DILLON WAS gone, Jacklyn eased herself as best she could away from the dead snake, putting her back to a warm rock. She prayed that her ankle wasn't broken, but the pain of just moving it almost made her black out again.

As Dillon disappeared from view, she felt a sob well up inside her, then surface. She swore, fighting back the urge to give in to the pain, to the despair. How was she going to be able to find the evidence now, let alone ride out of here?

Not only that, the receiver terminal for Dillon's tracking device was on her horse. This would be the perfect opportunity for him to take off. She couldn't very well chase after him. She couldn't even walk, and if he didn't return with her horse...

She looked up to see him leading both horses toward her, and relief made her weak. She was reminded of how gentle he'd been moments before as he'd checked her leg.

"You all right?" he asked, as he knelt down in front of her again.

She nodded, unable to speak around the lump in her throat. He had to have known she'd be worried he might not come back for her.

He reached out and brushed his fingers across her cheek. "Let me help you up on your horse."

She nodded and let him ease her up onto her good leg. His big hands were gentle as he put them around her waist and lifted her up into the saddle.

The cry escaped her lips even though she was fighting to keep it in as she tried to put her injured foot into the stirrup.

"Okay, you aren't going to be able to ride out of here," he said.

"No, I—"

"It's miles to the nearest ranch—and that ranch belongs to Shade Waters. You'd never make it. Anyway, it will be getting dark soon. We'll make camp for the night up there on that hill, and take the road out in the morning," he said, pointing to the southeast.

Clearly, he'd given this some thought already. She shook her head, close to tears. "I can ride. We have to tell someone about Reda."

Dillon pulled off his hat and raked a hand through his hair as he looked up at her. "Won't make any difference to Reda if we tell someone tonight or in the morning."

"You could ride out for help," she said through the pain.

"I'm not leaving you here alone. Tom Robinson is dead. So is Reda. The men behind this have nothing to lose now in killing anyone else who gets in their way."

She met his gaze.

He gave her a slow smile. "Finally starting to trust me? Scary, huh?"

Very. She looked toward the top of the bluff, where he planned to make camp. They would be able to see for miles up there. That's why he was insistent on camping on the spot, she realized. "You think they'll be back, don't you?"

"Let's just say I'm not taking any chances." He swung up into the saddle and looked over at her. "Come on. It's flat up there, with a few trees for shade and wood for a fire."

She wanted to argue, but as her horse began to move and she felt the pain in her ankle, she knew he was right. She wasn't going far. Nor could she leave here without evidence that would finally bring this rustling ring down.

As she let Dillon lead her up the steep bluff, she had one clear thought through the pain: her life was now literally in his hands.

Chapter Fourteen

The sun had dipped behind the mountains, leaving them a purple silhouette against the sunset. The air smelled of pine and aspens.

After Dillon had set up the tents and taken care of the horses, he made them dinner over a fire.

Jacklyn watched from where he'd settled her. He worked with efficiency, his movements sure, a man at home in this environment.

She felt herself relax as she watched him. The world seemed faraway, almost as if it no longer existed. Plus the pills he'd given her hadn't hurt.

"Looks like you're always prepared," Dillon had said when he'd found pain pills in the first aid kit she'd brought along with the other supplies.

"I try to be," she'd said, but in truth nothing could have prepared her for Dillon Savage.

A breeze stirred the leaves of the aspen grove where he'd chosen to camp. She stared at his broad back, surprised how protective he was.

"I feel so helpless," she said as he handed her a plate.

"It gives me a chance to wow you with my culinary talents, since dancing is out."

She tasted the simple food she'd brought and looked up at him in surprise. "It's wonderful."

He smiled, obviously pleased. "I had a lot of practice cooking over a fire." He sat down beside her with his own plate. She ate as if it had been days since she'd last tasted food.

He laughed. "I love a woman with a good appetite."

The fire crackled softly, filling the air with a warm glow as blackness settled around them. A huge sky overhead began to blink on as, one after another, stars popped out in the great expanse.

"I've lived in town for too long," she said, leaning back to gaze up at them. She found the Big Dipper, the constellation that had always been her guide since her father had first pointed it out to her as a child.

"This was the part I liked best," Dillon said from beside her.

She knew he was talking about his rustling days. He'd stayed in the wilds, seldom going into a town for anything except supplies. Or maybe to see some woman.

Mostly, she knew, he'd killed what he needed for food. Illegally, of course. She'd found enough of his camps, the coals still warm and the scent of wild meat in the air, but Dillon had always been miles away by that time.

"You know when I left here to go away to college, I never thought I'd come back," Dillon said. "Too many bad memories."

"Halsey's death," she said.

He nodded. "I thought I wouldn't miss Montana. But then, I always thought the ranch would be there if I ever changed my mind."

She glanced over at him, hearing his pain, remembering her own. After she'd left for college, her parents had divorced and gone their separate ways, the life she'd known, her childhood home and her family, dissolving.

She and Dillon fell into a comfortable silence, the fire popping softly, the breeze rustling the pine boughs and carrying the sweet scents of the land below them.

DILLON WAS SURPRISED when Jacklyn began to tell him about her parents, the divorce, the new families they'd made, how hard it was to accept the changes, to bond with the strangers that were suddenly her family.

He sat quietly as she opened up to him. Then he talked about Halsey, something he never did.

But it was a night for confidences, he decided. A night for clearing the air between them. Here, on this high bluff, they weren't an ex-con rustler and a stock detective. They had no shared past. They were just a man and a woman, both with histories they wanted to let go of.

Their talk turned to more pleasant things, like growing up in Montana. Both had spent most of their time as kids wading through creeks, climbing rocks and trees, daydreaming under a canopy of stars.

As the fire burned down, he saw there were tears in Jack's eyes. "How's the ankle?"

"Better."

He couldn't tell if she was lying or not. "Cold?"

She shook her head, her gaze holding his.

"I better check the horses," he said, dragging his eyes away as he got to his feet. She dropped her gaze as well, but he could still feel the warmth of it as he walked down the steep slope to the creek. The horses were fine, just as he knew they would be.

His real reason for coming down here was to make sure the area was secure. Earlier he'd rigged a few devices that would warn him if anyone tried to come up the bluff tonight. He didn't like surprises and he couldn't shake the bad feeling that had settled in his belly the minute he saw Reba Harper's shotgun lying beside the rock pile.

JACKLYN STARED INTO the fire. Sparks rose from the flames, sending fiery light into the air like fireflies. She could feel the effects of the pills Dillon had given her, but she knew they weren't responsible for the way she was feeling about him.

No, just before the rattlesnake had lunged, before Dillon had killed it, before she'd taken the pills, she'd acknowledged she would have only one regret if she were to die at that moment.

When Dillon touched her shoulder, she jumped. She hadn't heard him return.

"Sorry. I didn't mean to scare you." He threw some more wood on the fire.

She gazed into the flames again, too aware of him as he sat down beside her. Her heart was pounding, and all the oxygen seemed to be sucked up by the fire.

"You're trembling," he said softly, his breath stirring the hair at her temple. "Your ankle is worse than you said."

"No, it's not my ankle," she managed to say around the lump in her throat. She turned her face up to the stars, feeling free out here, as if there were no rules. Was that how Dillon had felt? With society so far away, was it as if that life didn't exist? "Dillon…"

"We should get some sleep," he said, rising to his feet.

She grabbed his shirtsleeve and pulled him back down to her, landing her mouth on his.

He let out a soft chuckle. "What do you think you're doing?"

"I'm seducing you," she said, and began to unbutton his shirt.

He placed a hand over hers, stopping her. "I don't think that's a good idea."

"I do." She unbuttoned her own shirt and let it slide off her shoulders.

SHADE WATERS HEARD the creak of the barn door. The ranch hands were all in town, a little treat he'd given them for the night. He listened to the soft, stealthy movements and waited.

He'd thought it would take longer. He smiled to himself and felt his eyes flood, the bittersweet rush of being right.

"Dad?" Nate's voice was tenuous. "Shade?" he called a little louder. "We need to talk."

Shade gave himself a little longer.

"Dad, I know you're in here," Nate said, irritation mixing with the anxiety.

Shade was just glad Elizabeth wasn't here to see the kind of man her son had turned into. Or what lengths Nate would go to. Or for that matter, Shade himself.

"I'm back here," he finally called, and waited. He'd purposely sat on the bench next to the tack room. The only light was the overhead one a few yards down the aisle. He liked being in the dark as Nate came toward him, his son's face illuminated in the harsh yellow light, his in shadow.

"We need to talk."

"There isn't anything to talk about. I've made up my mind."

Nate stopped a few yards from him and didn't seem to know what to do with his hands. He finally stuck them into the back pockets of his jeans and shifted nervously from boot to boot. He looked young and foolish. He looked afraid.

"I know you don't want to cut me out of your will."

"No, I don't," Shade admitted. "But I'm going to."

"This is about Morgan, isn't it?"

"No, Nate, it's more about you."

"What can I say to you to make you change your mind?"

Shade shook his head. "You wanted Morgan. You have her. Or did you get her only because she thought that the W Bar would be hers someday?"

Nate glared at him, fury in his eyes. "You think I can't get a woman without buying her with *your* money?"

Shade said nothing. The answer was too obvious.

"Can't we at least talk about this?" Nate's voice broke.

"There's nothing to talk about, Nate. You made your bed. Now lie in it."

"Like you made your bed when you cheated on my mother?" Nate snapped.

Waters saw an image of Reda Harper flash in his mind. She'd been so young, so beautiful and alive, so trusting. He would never forgive himself for what he'd done to her. He'd made her the angry, bitter woman she was today.

"I gave her up for you boys and your mother." He turned away, hoping that was the end of it.

"Do you think monsters are made or born?"

Waters turned back to stare at his son. "Are you crazy?"

Nate laughed. "Crazy? I'm just like you."

"You're nothing like me," Waters snapped.

"Oh, you might be surprised."

"I doubt that," he said. "Nothing you could do would surprise me."

"How could I not be like you? All these years of watching the way you just took whatever you wanted. You didn't think I knew." Tears welled in his eyes. "You made me who I am today."

Shade felt sick just looking at his son.

"I only wanted something of my own. Morgan—" His voice broke and he sounded close to tears.

"For hell's sake, if you wanted something of your own why would you marry a woman who's been with half the men in the county, including Dillon Savage?" Shade demanded.

Nate nodded, smiling through his tears. "I have to ask you since I won't get another chance. If Halsey had died before you hooked up with Reda Harper…"

"What are you trying to say?" Waters demanded, knowing exactly where Nate was going with this.

"You would have left me and Mom, wouldn't you?"

The big rancher rose to his feet. "I've heard enough of this. A man has to make sacrifices in this life. You need to learn that." He couldn't help the bitterness he heard in his voice. How could he explain true love to a man who'd just married a woman like Morgan Landers?

Nor could he tell Nate what giving up Reda had cost him. That he still regretted it every day of his life and would take that regret to his grave with him. And maybe worse, he'd had to let her go on hating him, let her go on believing that he'd only been after her ranch all those years ago, that he'd never loved her.

Nate would never understand that kind of loss. But he would someday, when Shade was dead and couldn't walk up the road to the mailbox to get the letters in the faded lavender envelopes, trying to keep his secrets.

"So what would you like me to sacrifice?" Nate asked. "Morgan? Maybe my life? Because you and I both know that I will never measure up to Halsey, will I, *Dad?* Isn't that what this is about? Halsey."

"I loved Halsey. He was my son." Just saying his son's name made him ache inside.

"Admit it," Nate said, stepping closer. "If you had the choice, if you could wave your hand through the air and change everything, you'd want it to be me who died instead of my brother."

There it was. "Yes," Shade said, and looked away in shame.

SHE WAS BEAUTIFUL, the black lacy bra cupping her perfect breasts, her skin creamy and smooth. Dillon felt an ache in his belly and felt himself go instantly hard.

Leaning down, he brushed his lips across hers. "Jack, do you have any idea what the sight of you half-naked is doing to me?"

She grinned in the firelight. "I noticed, actually."

"Does this mean you trust me?" he had to ask as he looked into her eyes.

"With my life," she said.

He laughed and shook his head. "I just wanted you to believe that I wasn't behind the rustling. I'm not sure you should trust me with your life, Jack," he added seriously.

"Too late. I already have," she said, and he saw naked desire in her gray eyes.

It was the last thing he expected. And, he realized, the only thing he wanted. "Jack—"

She pulled him to her and kissed him. He dropped to his knees in front of her, being careful not to brush against her hurt ankle as he took her in his arms and kissed her the way he'd been wanting to since the first time he'd laid eyes on her.

Damn, but this woman had gotten in his blood. For the past four years he'd told himself he wanted to get even with her. But as usual, he'd been lying to himself.

He just wanted Jacklyn Wilde. Wanted her in his arms. Wanted her in his bed. He drew back from the kiss to trail a finger over her lips as he searched her eyes, his heart beating too fast.

"There's no going back," he said as he un-buckled her gun belt. "Unlike you, I take no prisoners."

JACKLYN FELT HER BLOOD run hot as he drew his palm down her throat to her breasts. She leaned back, closing her eyes as she felt his fingers slip aside the lace of her bra, his touch warm and gentle.

Her eyes flew open, heat rushing to her center, when he traced around her rock-hard nipple, then bent to suck it through the thin lace, his mouth as hot as the fire he'd started inside her.

She arched against his mouth, wanting him as she had never wanted anything in her life.

He scooped her up in his arms and carried her to one of the small tents, setting her gently down inside it and crawling in after her.

She could see the firelight glowing through the thin nylon, could still smell the smoke and the pines. It was cold in the tent, but in Dillon's arms she instantly warmed.

He unhooked her bra, baring her breasts to his touch. She hurriedly unbuttoned his shirt, desperate to feel his chest against hers, skin to skin. It was hard and hot, just as she knew it would be.

His hand slipped under her waistband and she gasped as he touched her, finding her wet and ready. Their eyes met. Slowly he unbuttoned her jeans.

"We have to leave your boot on," he said. "I've never made love to a woman wearing her boots. But you know me, I'm up for anything." His smile faded. "Are you sure this won't be too painful?"

She grabbed his shoulders and pulled him down in answer. He wrapped his arms around her and kissed her, teasing her tongue with his, his movements slow and purposeful, as if they had all night. They did.

IT WAS ALMOST DAYLIGHT when Dillon heard a sound and sat up with a start. They'd left the tent flap open. He could see the cold embers in the fire pit and smell the smoke as a light wind stirred the ashes and rustled the leaves on the nearby trees.

But he knew that wasn't what he'd heard. Someone was out there.

Feeling around in the darkness, he found Jack's weapon and slid it from the holster, careful not to wake her. He could hear her breathing softly and was reminded of their lovemaking. Desire for her hit him like a fist. He would never get enough of her even if he lived to be a hundred.

He edged away from her warm body with

reluctance, not wanting to leave her even for a moment. Stopping at the door, he leaned back to brush a kiss over her bare hip, and then rose and stepped from the tent.

Reaching back in, he withdrew his jeans and boots, then put them on, tucking the pistol into the waistband of his pants as he straightened and listened.

Just as he'd feared, he heard a limb snap below him on the hillside. He'd set up some small snare traps to warn him if anyone approached their camp, and knew that was what had awakened him. Now it sounded as if someone was trying to make his way up the slope.

It would be light soon, but Dillon knew he couldn't wait. The noise he'd heard could have been made by an animal. There were deer and antelope here, and smaller creatures that could have released one of the traps.

But his instincts told him this animal was larger and more cunning. This one would find a way up the steep bluff. Unless Dillon stopped him.

How had someone found them so quickly?

He could only assume that one of Waters's men had seen where they'd driven across the pasture. Once they found the hidden truck, they would tell Waters. And he would know exactly where they were headed.

Dillon heard one of the horses whinny. He thought about waking Jack. All he wanted to do was get back to bed with her as quickly as possible. And maybe he was wrong. Maybe there was nothing to worry about.

Moving through the trees, he headed toward the creek and the horses. If someone had found them, he'd be smart enough to take their mounts. It was much easier to run down a man on foot.

As he neared the creek, Dillon stopped to listen again. Not a sound. Was it possible it had just been the wind in the trees? Moving on down the bluff, he saw both horses were still tied to the rope he'd strung between two tree trunks beside the narrow stream. The animals would be reacting if there were any other horses around. But probably not to a man on foot.

Dillon tried to convince himself that everything was fine. And yet as he started to turn, he felt a rush of apprehension. He couldn't wait to get back to Jack.

"Dillon." The voice was soft. One of the horses whinnied again, moving to one side.

In the dim light of morning, Dillon watched Buford Cole step from the shadows. He'd wondered why Buford was going out to Waters's place when he'd seen him earlier. Now he had a pretty good idea.

"You work for Waters." Dillon's words carried all of his contempt.

Buford chuckled, still keeping one of the horses between him and Dillon. "Put down the gun and we can talk about it."

"Doesn't seem like there is much to say," Dillon commented, his heart in his throat. Had Buford come alone? Not likely. Dillon glanced back up the bluff toward the camp.

"She's fine. I thought you and I should talk."

"Too bad you didn't want to talk in town, where we could have sat down with a beer," Dillon said.

"I'm serious, Dillon. Put down the gun and make this easy on both of us."

The last thing he wanted to do was make things easy for Buford. He brought the gun up fast, knowing he would probably only get one shot. Unless he missed his guess, Buford would be armed.

Dillon fired just a split second before he

was struck from behind. He tumbled head-
long toward the creek, out before he even hit
the ground.

JACKLYN CAME AWAKE instantly, sitting up in
the tent and reaching for Dillon as she tried
to make sense of what she'd just heard. A
gunshot?

The bedroll beside her was empty, but still
warm. Dillon was gone, but he hadn't been
for long.

Her pulse raced as she scrambled in the
semidarkness of dawn to find her holster. Her
heart fell even though she'd known what she
was going to find. The holster was empty.

Where was Dillon? Her pulse took off at a
gallop. The gunshot. Oh God. He would have
returned to her if he could have. Her heart
was pounding so hard in her ears she almost
didn't hear it.

A limb cracked below her on the steep
bluff. She froze. A squirrel chattered off in
the distance. A bird belted out a short song
in a tree directly overhead. One of the horses
whinnied. Another answered.

Move! Move!

As she hurriedly pulled on her jeans, she
was reminded of her injured ankle. Thank God

it wasn't broken. But it was badly sprained. She wasn't sure she could walk on it. What was she saying? She had no choice.

She pulled on her shirt and other boot. Dillon. She fought the tears that burned her eyes. She'd gotten him into this.

And if he was still alive, she would get him out. She dug in her saddlebag and found the second gun she always carried, and her knife. Then, as quietly as possible, she cut a slit in the back of the tent and taking the tracking monitor in its case, crawled out. She continued to crawl until she reached the trees before she managed to get painfully to her feet.

Her ankle hurt, but not as much as her heart. She wanted to call to Dillon, except she knew that would only let whoever was out there know exactly where she was. Dillon wouldn't answer, anyway. If he could, he would have returned to the tent for her.

A little voice at the back of her mind taunted that she was wrong about him. That he was the leader of the rustling ring. That he'd gotten her out here for more than a romp in the tent.

She told the voice to shut up, checked the gun and considered her options. They weren't great. Her first instinct was to head in the direction of the horses. She had a pretty good idea that was where whoever had come into camp would be found, given that the horses sounded restless.

That was where she suspected she would find Dillon.

As much as she wanted to find him, she was smart enough to know whoever was out there was counting on her appearing. Waiting down there for her. Figuring she would hear the gunshot and come to investigate.

It would be full light soon. She had to move fast. She worked her way back through the trees, in the opposite direction from the horses. The going was slow and painful, the ground steep.

When she reached the bottom of the bluff, she stopped in a stand of trees. Opening the case, she took out the receiver terminal, listened to make sure she was still alone, and turned it on.

The steady beep of the tracking monitor filled her with relief even as she reminded herself it didn't mean that Dillon was alive.

But at least now she knew where he was.

Chapter Fifteen

Dillon came up out of the darkness slowly. His head hurt like hell and for a moment he forgot where he was. He was so used to waking up in a prison cell that at first he thought he was dreaming. Especially when he saw Buford standing over him.

Dillon groaned and, holding his head, sat up. As he felt his skull and found the lump where someone had hit him, his memory gradually started to come back to him.

"What the hell's going on, Buford?" he demanded, taking in the gun in his old friend's hand—and the fact that the barrel was pointed at his chest.

"You should have stayed in prison."

"I'm getting that," Dillon said. "Look, I don't know who else is with you, but don't hurt Wilde, okay?"

"So it's like that," Buford said with a smirk.

"You know, I misjudged you." Dillon's mind was racing. He knew he'd never be able to get to his feet fast enough to jump Buford before he caught a bullet in the chest. But he had to think of something.

"Misjudged me?" Buford kept looking up toward the camp. Dillon was betting that whoever had hit him had gone there looking for Jack.

"I never figured you for the leader of this rustling ring. Frankly, I never thought you were smart enough. I guess I was wrong." The moment the words were out of his mouth, Dillon saw that Buford *wasn't* the man giving the orders. So did that mean whoever had gone up the bluff was?

"Just shut up," Buford snapped. "Too bad he didn't hit you harder."

"Yeah." Dillon reached back again to rub the bump on his head. "You know, I've always wanted to ask you, were you the one who set me up the day Wilde caught me?"

Buford had always been a lousy poker player. Too much showed in his face. Just like right now.

"Well, that solves that mystery." Dillon kept his voice light, but his heart was pounding. It was all he could do not to lunge at his old friend and take his chances.

"You were always such an arrogant bastard," Buford said.

Dillon nodded in agreement, even though it hurt his head, as everything became clear to him. "It's because I wanted to stop rustling cattle, wasn't it."

"You get us involved and then you want to quit just when we're starting to make some money," Buford said, anger in his voice.

Dillon stared at him, a bad feeling settling in his stomach. "You didn't put all the cattle on the W Bar like I told you to."

"What was the point? No one gave a crap about your warped attempt at your so-called justice. Waters bought out my family's ranch just like he did yours. You didn't see me losing sleep over it. The only reason I'd risk rustling cattle was if there was real money in it and not what you paid us to help."

Dillon let that settle in for a moment. It explained a lot. Buford, Pete Barclay and Arlen Dubois had seemed guilty when he'd seen them. Now he understood why. He'd thought it was because they'd set him up. As it turned out, they'd done that, too—and double-crossed him.

"I've gotta know. Halsey's good-luck coin…I'm betting you took it from his pocket at the funeral."

"You'd lose that bet," Buford said.

Then who? "So who do I have to thank for this lump on my head? Pete?" Buford's expression told him it hadn't been Pete. *"Arlen?"*

"I told you to shut up."

Dillon frowned. If it really hadn't been either of them, who did that leave?

"Where's your girlfriend?" a very familiar voice asked, from directly behind him. Dillon felt his skin crawl, and heard Buford chuckle at his obvious surprise.

AS JACKLYN WORKED HER WAY around the rock bluff, the sun broke over the horizon. She would have less cover and more chance of being seen before she discovered what she had to fear.

The wind in the trees sounded like ocean waves. Past the trees, she spotted a pond, its surface pitching and rolling, the chop cresting white as it beat against the shoreline. The wind whistled past her, too, tossing her hair into her eyes.

Last night Dillon had taken out her braid…. Just the memory made her weak. His fingers in her hair… The two of them had made love through the night with an intimacy that she'd never experienced before. There was only one way she could explain it. Love.

The wind groaned in the pine boughs, whistling through the branches, making it impossible to hear if someone was sneaking up on her.

She pushed on through the tall grass. The sky stretched overhead, a pale blue canvas empty of clouds. But the wind had a bite to it.

She stopped to listen, the wind seeming to be her only companion. Ahead was another stand of pines, dark green. She had to be getting near the creek. Near where she believed Dillon had left the horses. She didn't dare check the monitor again.

Angling down the mountain through the pines, she came across a smaller pond nearly hidden in the trees. There, with the dense pines acting as a windbreak, the surface was slick and calm. She stopped to listen, hearing the wind sigh among the treetops.

A track in the soft mud at the edge caught her eye. She stepped closer, crouching down to study the multitude of animal prints. In the middle of the deer and antelope tracks was the clear imprint of a boot heel.

She froze as she heard something other than wind in pine boughs. The water beside her mirrored the sky, the dark green of the trees towering over her. Something moved in the reflection.

She jerked back, her eyes on the pines, the fallen needles a bed at her feet. Even over the wind, she heard the soft rustle. Not of swaying branches, but something advancing through the grass, moving with purpose.

She unsnapped her holster and rested her palm on the butt of the pistol as she moved, just as purposefully, around the pond.

The wind whipped through the pines, sending a shower of dust over her. She froze, blinded for one terrifying instant.

Her prey had stopped, as well. A strange silence fell over the landscape. Shadows played at the edge of the water.

She started to take a step toward the cool shade in the pines as it burst from the trees. All she saw was the frantic flutter of wings. She didn't remember pulling the pistol, her heart lurching, her breath catching. The thunder of blood in her ears as the grouse flew past was too much like the heart-stopping buzz of the rattlesnake.

Jacklyn sucked in a breath, then another,

her hand shaking as she slid the pistol back in the holster. But she kept her hand on the cool, smooth butt, her eyes on the trees ahead.

He was here. She could feel him. Unconsciously, she lifted her head and sniffed the air. Crickets began to chirp again in the grass. Somewhere off to her left a meadowlark sang a refrain. Closer, the grass rustled again with movement.

Once in the awning of the trees, she saw the game trail. It wound through the pines, disappearing in shadow. She stopped, crouched and touched the soft damp earth.

Another boot print.

Few people ever knew this kind of eerie silence. Solitude coupled with an acute aloneness. A feeling of being far from anything and anyone who mattered to her. Entirely on her own. She'd been here before. Fighting not only a country wrought with dangers, but also men—the most dangerous adversaries of all.

Tracking required stealth, so as not to warn other animals of her presence. She'd walked up on her share of bears, the worst a grizzly sow with two cubs. The mother grizzly had let out a whoof, but the warning came too late.

The sow's hair had stood up on her neck as she rose on her hind legs, even as Jacklyn slowly began to back away. Then the sow had charged.

Jacklyn knew that running was the worst thing she could do, but in that instant it was a primal survival instinct stronger than any she'd ever felt. Fortunately, her training had kicked in. She'd dropped to the ground, curled into a fetal position and covered her head with one arm as she slipped her other hand down to the bear spray clipped to her belt.

The spray had saved her life.

Just as she hoped the gun would today, because whoever, whatever, was after her was nearby now.

MORGAN LANDERS MOVED around to stand in front of Dillon, flashing him one of her smiles. "I lied about hoping I wouldn't see you again."

"It seems that's not the only thing you lied about," Dillon said. He'd always thought he wouldn't put anything past Morgan, but he was having a hard time believing she'd been the one to coldcock him. He had a sizable lump on his head. Morgan must have one hell of a swing. Unless it had been someone else.

He felt a sliver of worry stab into him as he realized that Morgan had just come from the camp on top of the bluff. "See Wilde while you were up there?" he asked, tilting his head toward the camp.

Morgan's gaze said she had guessed how close he was with the stock detective, and didn't like it. Too bad for Morgan. "As a matter of fact, she seems to be missing."

Dillon felt his heart soar. Jack had heard the shot, and being Jack, she'd known what to do.

Buford swore. "So what are you doing here? Go find her."

Morgan sent him a bored look. "It's being taken care of."

Jack was out there somewhere. She would need an advantage, because from what Dillon could see, there were at least three of them, maybe more. And as far as he knew she wasn't armed. But Jack being Jack she'd have a second gun he didn't know about.

What was also clear was that whoever was running this show wasn't going to let them out of this alive.

"Being taken care of by your boss?" Dillon asked Morgan.

"I don't have a boss," she snapped.

"Right. I could believe Buford was running

this rustling ring easier than I could you, Morgan."

"You know, Dillon, you always were a bastard," she said, stepping closer.

He grinned at her. "And you, Morgan, were always a greedy, coldhearted bitch."

She lunged at him as if to slap his face. Buford yelled for her to stop, but Dillon was pretty sure she didn't hear him—or didn't care.

He grabbed her arm, using it as leverage as he pulled himself up, then swung her around in front of him for cover as he propelled her into Buford, knocking him off balance.

Buford's gun went off with a loud boom that echoed in the trees as the three of them, locked in a tangle of limbs, went down.

JACKLYN FROZE as the sound of the gun report filled the air. Her heart lodged in her throat. Not knowing if Dillon was alive or dead was killing her.

Worse, that little voice in the back of her head kept taunting her, trying to make her lose faith in him, telling her it was him stalking her through the trees.

As the gunshot blast died away, she heard

the rustle of grass, the crack of a limb and knew he'd circled around her and was now right behind her.

Jacklyn took a breath and turned, her weapon coming up and her mind screaming: *Who are you about to kill?*

He stood just a few feet from her. She could see both of his hands. He appeared to be unarmed. He looked confused, almost lost.

"Nate?"

"What happened to you?" Nate asked, having apparently noticed her limp.

"I sprained my ankle." This felt surreal, as if she was dreaming all of it. She held the gun on him, but he didn't seem to care.

"Any luck catching those rustlers?" he asked, his voice sounding strange, almost as if he was trying not to laugh.

She tightened her hold on the gun. "Nate, what are you doing here?"

"Looking for you. Dillon told me to find you and bring you back to camp."

"Why didn't he come himself?"

"He's hurt."

Her breath rushed out of her. "How did he get hurt?"

Nate shrugged.

"Is it bad?" she asked, her heart beating so hard her chest hurt.

"You'd have to be the judge of that," he said. She wondered if he'd been drinking. She'd never seen him like this.

"Nate, what's going on?" she pressed, the way she might ask a mental patient.

He tilted his head as if he heard a voice calling him.

She heard nothing. "Are you here alone?"

"Who would be here with me?" he asked, as if amused.

"I thought Shade might have come with you," she said.

"Oh, that's right, you haven't heard. My father was murdered last night in his barn."

DILLON ROLLED OVER, trying to catch his breath. He felt as if he'd been punched in the chest, all the air knocked from his lungs. His hand went there and came away sticky with blood. He'd been hit.

But after a moment, he realized it wasn't his blood. It was Morgan's.

She lay on her back, staring vacantly up at the morning sky. Her shirt was bright red, soaked with blood.

Dillon tried to get up, but Buford was already on his feet and holding the gun. The cowboy kicked at his head. Dillon managed to evade him, taking only a glancing blow, as he rolled over and came up in a sitting position, his back to a tree.

"You stupid bastard," Buford swore. "You stupid bastard."

Dillon focused on him, hearing the fear in the man's voice. Buford was pacing in front of him, clearly wanting to shoot him. Had whoever Buford took orders from told him not to kill Dillon?

But looking into his old friend's eyes, he saw that change. Buford raised the gun, pointing it into Dillon's face. "You're a dead man."

JACKLYN STARED AT NATE in shock. Shade Waters murdered? "That's horrible. Do they know who—"

"Sheriff McCray has put out an APB. I hate to be the one to tell you this, but I saw Dillon Savage running away from the barn right before I found my father's body."

All the air rushed out of her as if she'd been hit. "Nate, that's not possible. Dillon was with me last night."

He shrugged. "I guess you'll have to sell

that to Sheriff McCray, but since Dillon made his getaway in your state truck, the sheriff thinks you might have been an accomplice."

"What? Nate…" She felt fear seize her. "Nate, that's crazy. No one will ever believe it."

"No? Well, the sheriff says the only reason you got Savage out of jail is that you have something for him. And everyone knows he's the one who's been headin' up this gang of rustlers. I'm betting the rustling will stop once he's back in prison."

She stared at Nate Waters as if she'd never seen him before. She'd never seen *this* man, and he frightened her more than if he had been holding a gun on her.

"You must be in shock," she said, realizing that had to be what was going on.

He laughed as if that was the funniest thing he'd ever heard. "You know my father always blamed me for Halsey's death. Dillon thought he blamed him, but he was wrong. I was the one holding the rope on that horse that day. I killed Halsey. His luck had finally run out. So I took his good-luck coin after I saw Dillon put it in my brother's suit jacket at the funeral."

The good-luck coin found near where Tom Robinson was attacked. Nate Waters had just implicated himself. "Nate, why don't you take me to Dillon," she said, trying to keep her voice even.

"Not until you put down your gun, Ms. Wilde."

"I can't do that." Even though Nate didn't appear armed, he was talking crazy. If anything he was saying was true, then he was responsible for the rustling, for the attack on Tom Robinson, the death of Reda Harper and… Jacklyn felt sick. And apparently the death of his father, Shade Waters.

"The thing is, if you don't drop the gun, I'm going to give my men orders to kill Dillon," Nate said. "His blood will be on your hands."

His men? How many were there? "Nate, why would you do that?"

The smile never reached his eyes. "I think you already know the answer to that. The gun, Ms. Wilde. Drop it and step away."

She didn't move. She had to get to Dillon. But without a weapon, she knew they were both dead.

"Buford?" Nate called.

"Yeah." The answer came from the trees behind Nate.

"Everything all right over there?" Nate asked.

"Yeah. Just a little accident, but everything's okay."

Jacklyn recognized Buford Cole's voice and could tell that things were definitely not all right. She hated to think what that last gunshot was about.

"Well?" Nate asked her with an odd tilt of his head. "You want me to give the order?"

"How do I know Dillon isn't already dead?"

"Dillon?" Nate called.

Silence, then a surprised-sounding Dillon said, "Nate?" as if he'd been trying to place the voice, since it had to be the last one he'd expected to hear out here.

"Dillon," Jack called to him.

"Jack!" His response came back at once.

She heard so much in that one word that tears burned her eyes. "Are you all right?"

"He won't be if you say one more word to him," Nate said in that calm, frightening voice.

DILLON TOOK A DEEP BREATH, weak with relief. Jack was alive and Buford seemed to be using every ounce of his self-control not to pull the trigger on the gun he was holding on him.

The overwhelming relief was quickly replaced with the realization that Jack was with Nate. And Buford seemed to be losing it by the minute.

So Shade Waters was behind the rustling, just as Dillon had thought. He found little satisfaction in being right though. Shade was dangerous enough. But apparently, he'd sent Nate to tie up some loose ends. Nate was unpredictable. Maybe even a little unstable. No way was this going to end well.

"Oh man, I can't believe this," Buford said again as he began to pace back and forth again, always keeping the gun aimed in Dillon's direction. He looked more than nervous; he looked scared to death. Unfortunately, it only made him more dangerous.

"I can't believe she's dead," he said, raking his free hand through his hair. His hat had fallen off during the skirmish, but he didn't seem to have noticed.

"I think you'd better tell me what's going on," Dillon said, trying to keep his voice calm. "What's Nate doing with Jack?"

"You've messed everything up," Buford said, sounding as if he might break down at any minute. "You killed Morgan. What's

Nate going to do when he sees that you killed
Morgan? Hell, man, he married her. They
were going to go on their honeymoon."

"*You* pulled the trigger," Dillon said. "I
didn't kill her. You did."

Buford stopped pacing. His eyes had gone
wild, and he looked terrified of what Nate
Waters was going to do to him. Nate Waters,
a kid they'd all teased because he'd been such
a big crybaby.

Dillon felt bad about that now. Worse,
because he had a feeling that Nate Waters
was going to kill him. He just didn't want the
same thing to happen to Jack. He tried to
think fast, but his head ached and Buford was
standing over him with a gun, acting like a
crazy person.

"You'd better let me help you," Dillon said.
"Nate's obviously going to be upset about
his wife." Dillon avoided looking at Morgan,
lying dead on the ground. Even though she
was obviously in this up to her sweet little
neck, she didn't deserve to die like this.

Buford was right about one thing. Things
were messed up big time.

"I'm telling you, Buford, for old times'
sake, let me help you."

The man looked as if he might be considering it, so Dillon rushed on. "Come on, old buddy. Things are messed up if you're taking orders from Nate Waters, anyway. Whatever he's gotten you into, Jack and I can help cut you a deal. But if you wait and he kills anyone else—"

"There a problem here, Buford?" Nate asked as he came out of the trees, holding a gun on Jack.

Dillon groaned inwardly. A few more minutes and he might have been able to turn Buford. Now there was no hope of that.

"It was an accident," Buford said. "Man, I'm so sorry. I…"

Nate pushed Jack over by Dillon. She dropped to the ground next to him and he put his arm around her. He could see that she was scared, and her ankle had to be killing her. But he knew Jack, knew she was strong and determined. And with her beside him, he told himself, they had a chance of surviving this. She owed him a dance. Kind of.

Mostly, he couldn't bear the thought that they'd found each other, two people from worlds apart, only to have some jackass like Nate Waters kill them.

Nate walked over to where Morgan lay dead on the ground.

Dillon heard a small wounded sound come out of Jack. He pulled her closer and whispered, "It's going to be okay."

Buford was pacing again, swinging the gun around. "Oh man, Nate, I'm so sorry. It was an accident. Dillon, man, it's his fault. You told me not to shoot him, but he jumped me. Morgan… Oh man."

"Shut up," Nate said, sounding close to tears. "She was just a greedy bitch who slept with anyone and everyone."

"She was your *wife*," Buford said, obviously before he could think.

Nate turned to glare at him. "She tricked me into marrying her. I don't want a woman who's been with Dillon Savage."

Oh, boy, here it comes, Dillon thought, as Nate swung the gun in his hand toward Dillon's head. Next to him, he felt Jack press something hard against his thigh. Apparently she'd taken it from one of her boots.

A knife.

He slipped his arm from around her. "What? This is about Morgan Landers?" He shook his head and sat up a little, dropping his hands to the ground next to him. "Come on. There has to be more to it than that."

Nate stepped closer. "What would you know about it? You have any concept what it's like to grow up with Shade Waters as a father? To live your whole life in the shadow of the great Halsey Waters? You have no idea."

"So all this is to show your father," Dillon said, closing his hand around the knife handle hidden beneath his thigh. If Nate came any closer…

"It was bad enough that he idolized Halsey but when you started rustling cattle to pay back the ranchers who you felt had wronged you…" Nate took a breath and let it out on a sigh. "The bastard actually admired you the way you slipped those stolen cattle in among his." Waters's laugh held no humor. "You were a damn hero. Even the great stock detective here couldn't catch you. I was the one who put up the hundred thousand dollar reward for your capture from the money my mother left me. He never knew."

"Damn, I wish I had known that. I would have had my friend Buford here collect it." He looked past Nate. "But then he already had, huh?" Dillon remembered the truck Buford had been driving when he passed them, headed for the W Bar. It had been an expensive ride—not the kind of vehicle a man who works at the stockyards could afford. "So it really was you, Buford, who betrayed me."

Buford Cole had looked frightened before. Now he looked petrified. "Kill him. Just get it over. You said nobody knows where they are. We can bury them with the cattle. Morgan, too. No one will ever have to know."

Nate raised his gun, pointed it at Dillon's head. Unfortunately, Dillon wasn't close enough to reach him with the knife. Nor could he launch himself faster than a speeding bullet. He hoped his life didn't pass before his eyes before he died. He wasn't that proud of the things he'd done.

IT HAPPENED SO FAST that Jacklyn never saw it coming.

She'd buried the hand farthest away from Nate's view, grabbing a handful of fine dirt. She was planning to throw it in Nate's face, anything to give Dillon a chance to use the knife.

But as she raised her balled fist holding the dirt, Nate swung around and fired. He couldn't have missed in a million years. Not with Buford standing just feet behind him.

The bullet caught Buford Cole in the face. He went down with a thump.

But before he hit the ground Dillon was on his feet. He drove the knife into Nate's side.

It took Jacklyn a little longer to get to her one good foot. She hit Nate in the face with the dirt and wrestled her weapon from him.

"Nate Waters? You're under arrest for the murders of Buford Cole, Reda Harper, Morgan Landers—"

"Morgan *Waters*," he corrected, holding his side and looking down at the blood leaking between his fingers, as if he'd never seen anything quite so interesting.

"Shade Waters and the attack on Tom Robinson."

Nate looked up at her. "Tom died earlier this morning."

"The murder of Tom Robinson," she said, her voice breaking.

Nate looked up, his head tilted, as if again listening to something she couldn't hear.

After a moment, he smiled. "Halsey said to make sure they spell my name correctly in the paper. Too bad Shade isn't around to see it."

Epilogue

Jacklyn hesitated at the door. She could hear the band playing. Glancing at her reflection in the window, she ran a hand over her hair, feeling a little self-conscious.

Her hair was out of its braid and floating around her shoulders. She so seldom wore it down that her image in the glass looked like that of a stranger. A stranger with flushed cheeks and bright eyes. A stranger in love.

She felt like a schoolgirl as she pushed open the door to the community center. The dance was in full swing, the place crowded.

For a while there'd been shock, then sadness, then slowly, the community rallied, and pretty soon even the talk had died down. And there had been plenty of talk. The gossips kept the phone lines buzzing for weeks.

The first shock was Shade Waters's murder, followed by the news that his son Nate had confessed not only to killing him and the others, but also to having been behind all the cattle rustling.

Buford had been one of the rustlers Nate had hired but it was suspected that Pete Barclay and Arlen Dubois were also involved. Nate took full responsibility, though, for all the deaths and thefts, posing for reporters.

Jacklyn had wondered if he'd wished his father was alive to see it. Or had Nate told Shade everything before he killed him? She would never know.

On the heels of all the publicity came word that Shade Waters had been dying of cancer and had had but a few months to live, anyway. Everyone loved the irony of that, since few people had liked either Waters much.

The community had also taken Reda's death fairly well—especially when it came to light that she'd been blackmailing nearly half the county, including Shade Waters. For years, the sinners in the county had lived in fear of getting one of her letters, letting them know she knew their secrets and what it would take to keep her quiet.

But probably the news that had tongues

wagging the most was Shade Waters's will. He'd changed it, unknown to Nate, about the time that Nate had taken up with Morgan Landers. In the will, Shade left everything to the state except for one ranch—the former Savage Ranch. That he left to a boys' ranch for troubled teens, in his son Halsey's name.

"I thought you might not come," Dillon said behind Jacklyn, making her jump as the band broke into another song.

She turned slowly, feeling downright girlie in the slinky dress and high heels. She'd even put on a little makeup.

"Wow," he said, his blue eyes warming as he ran his fingers up her bare arms. "You look beautiful, Jack. But then I think you always look beautiful."

She smiled, pleased, knowing it was true. Dillon liked her in jeans and boots as much as he liked her in a dress. Mostly he liked her naked.

"You know, I didn't exactly win the bet," he said, feigning sheepishness.

"You said Waters was guilty. True, it wasn't the Waters you meant, but I'm not one to haggle over a bet," she said. "I just had to wait until my ankle was healed before I could pay up."

"Well, in that case, I guess you owe me a dance," he said as the band broke into a slow song.

She stepped into his arms, having missed being there even for a few hours. She looked up into his handsome face, wondering how she'd gotten by as long as she had without Dillon Savage in her life. The diamond ring he'd bought her glittered on her finger, his proposal still making her warm to her toes.

He'd bought a ranch up north, near a little town called Whitehorse, Montana. "I'm thinking we'll raise sheep. Nobody rustles sheep," he'd joked when he showed her the deed. "And babies. Lots of babies. I promise you I'm going to make you the happiest woman in northeastern Montana."

She'd laughed. But she was learning that Dillon Savage was good as his word. The man could dance. And he'd already made her happier than any woman in central Montana. She didn't doubt he'd live up to all his promises.

As he spun her around the room, she thought of the babies they would have, hoping they all looked like him. Except maybe the girls.

"You sorry?" he asked, his breath tickling her ear.

"About what?" She couldn't think of a single thing to be sorry for.

"I just thought you might be having second thoughts about settling down with me instead of chasing rustlers."

She smiled. "Darlin', there's only one rustler I want to be chasing."

"We can both stop running then. Because, Jack, you already caught him. The question now," he said with a grin, "is what you're going to do with him."

* * * * *

Happily ever after is just the beginning...

Turn the page for a sneak preview of
A HEARTBEAT AWAY
by
Eleanor Jones

*Harlequin Everlasting—Every great love
has a story to tell.™*
A brand-new series from Harlequin Books

Special? A prickle ran down my neck and my heart started to beat in my ears. Was today really special?

"Tuck in," he ordered.

I turned my attention to the feast that he had spread out on the ground. Thick, home-cooked-ham sandwiches, sausage rolls fresh from the oven and a huge variety of mouth-watering scones and pastries. Hunger pangs took over, and I closed my eyes and bit into soft homemade bread.

When we were finally finished, I lay back against the bluebells with a groan, clutching my stomach.

Daniel laughed. "Your eyes are bigger than your stomach," he told me.

I leaned across to deliver a punch to his arm, but he rolled away, and when my fist met fresh air I collapsed in a fit of giggles before relaxing on my back and staring up into the flawless blue sky. We lay like that for quite a while, Daniel and I, side by side in companionable silence, until he stretched out his hand in an arc that encompassed the whole area.

"Don't you think that this is the most beautiful place in the entire world?"

His voice held a passion that echoed my own feelings, and I rose onto my elbow and picked a buttercup to hide the emotion that clogged my throat.

"Roll over onto your back," I urged, prodding him with my forefinger. He obliged with a broad grin, and I reached across to place the yellow flower beneath his chin.

"Now, let us see if you like butter."

When a yellow light shone on the tanned skin below his jaw, I laughed.

"There…you do."

For an instant our eyes met, and I had the strangest sense that I was drowning in those honey-brown depths. The scent of bluebells engulfed me. A roaring filled my ears, and then, unexpectedly, in one smooth movement Daniel rolled me onto my back and plucked a buttercup of his own.

"And do *you* like butter, Lucy McTavish?" he asked. When he placed the flower against my skin, time stood still.

His long lean body was suspended over mine, pinning me against the grass. Daniel… dear, comfortable, familiar Daniel was suddenly bringing out in me the strangest sensations.

"Do you, Lucy McTavish?" he asked again, his voice low and vibrant.

My eyes flickered toward his, the whisper of a sigh escaped my lips and although a strange lethargy had crept into my limbs, I somehow felt as if all my nerve endings were on fire. He felt it, too—I could see it in his warm brown eyes. And when he lowered his face to mine, it seemed to me the most natural thing in the world.

None of the kisses I had ever experienced could have even begun to prepare me for the feel of Daniel's lips on mine. My entire body floated on a tide of ecstasy that shut out everything but his soft, warm mouth, and I knew that this was what I had been waiting for the whole of my life.

"Oh, Lucy." He pulled away to look into my eyes. "Why haven't we done this before?"

Holding his gaze, I gently touched his cheek, then I curled my fingers through the short thick hair at the base of his skull, over-whelmed by the longing to drown again in the sensations that flooded our bodies. And when his long tanned fingers crept across my tingling skin, I knew I could deny him nothing.

* * * * *

Be sure to look for
A HEARTBEAT AWAY,
available February 27, 2007.

And look, too, for
THE DEPTH OF LOVE
by Margot Early,
the story of a couple who must learn that
love comes in many guises—and
in the end it's the only thing that counts.

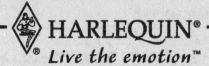

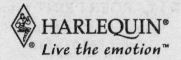

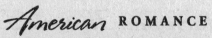
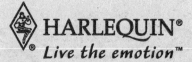

![Harlequin Historical logo] **Harlequin® Historical**
Historical Romantic Adventure!

*Imagine a time of chivalrous
knights and unconventional ladies,
roguish rakes and impetuous
heiresses, rugged cowboys
and spirited frontierswomen—
these rich and vivid tales will
capture your imagination!*

*Harlequin Historical . . .
they're too good to miss!*

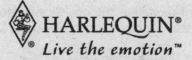

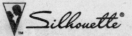